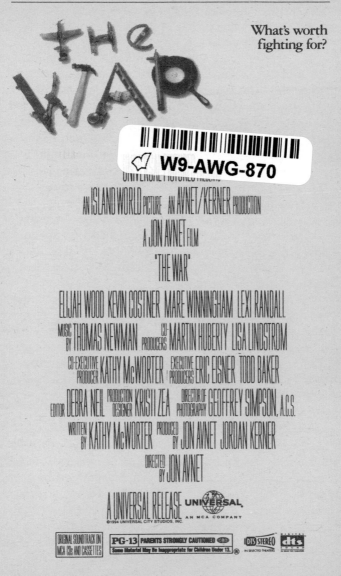

THE WAR

A Novel by
DEBORAH CHIEL
Based on a Motion Picture written by
KATHY McWORTER

JOVE BOOKS, NEW YORK

THE WAR

A Jove Book / published by arrangement with
MCA Publishing Rights

PRINTING HISTORY
Jove edition / November 1994

ISBN: 0-515-11447-2

A JOVE BOOK®
Jove Books are published by The Berkley Publishing Group,
200 Madison Avenue, New York, New York 10016.
JOVE and the "J" design are trademarks
belonging to Jove Publications, Inc.

PRINTED IN THE UNITED STATES OF AMERICA

10 9 8 7 6 5 4 3 2 1

For Neta Bolzman and Molly Krotick,
who know how to be good friends.

PROLOGUE

Ambertree, Mississippi, 1970

THE WOODS were overgrown, dense with foliage, hot and wet with humidity. Massive branches begrudgingly yielded to the forces of gravity, twisting, turning, reaching for the sunlight. The forest floor was covered with a thick rug of leaves, interspersed with hardy wild flowers—azaleas, black-eyed Susans, violets, wisteria, and primroses that grew with utter abandon in riotous shades of blue and yellow and red. These were ancient species of trees, immense and ageless, a jungle of cypresses and swamp hickories, maples and sycamores, magnolias and live oaks dripping with heavy mantles of thick Spanish moss.

This dark and secret place had a history of skirmishes fought, campaigns won and lost. General William Tecumseh Sherman led his men through these very woods when he marched across the state from Vicksburg to Meridian. His troops confiscated pigs and cows and horses for the use of the Union army. They burned houses and barns, churches and stores, laid waste to thousands of acres of cotton.

A hundred years had passed since then. The houses and barns had been rebuilt, the farms and cotton fields replanted. Herds of cows and horses now grazed in the fields where shots had once rang out and men had fallen defending the glorious ideals to which they had pledged their lives.

Times and circumstances had changed, yet much was the same. In Vietnam, a half a world away, another war was being fought in marshy fields and swampy forests. Young men were once again killing and being killed in battle while their leaders proclaimed the justice of their cause—the defense of freedom and democracy.

And in Mississippi, come summer, the magnolias still blossomed full creamy white and fruit-scented. Rabbits, squirrels, possum, and deer foraged for food in the woods, alert to the menacing sound of invading human footsteps. The local boys still ran wild through the forest, chasing one another among the trees, playing games of war in imitation of their elders.

Every day after school and on weekends when their chores were done, they came to the forest to wage combat. They had their special hiding places and weapons, strategies and secret codes, their whoops and war cries. The animals kept their distance, except for the occasional doe that ventured a few timid steps away from its mother to graze on the wild flowers. But even the doe knew to flee when an unfamiliar noise or a scent on the wind warned that the enemy was approaching.

The woods were full of danger. The Ambertree boys played hard and took no prisoners.

Those who were slower-footed, like Chet Ledindecker, who was huskier than the others, rarely eluded their pursuers. But today, determined to lose the soldiers who were hot on his heels, Chet was pushing himself to run faster. His hair was matted with sweat and he was breathing hard through his mouth. He dodged trees and sticker bushes as he crashed toward the safety zone at the far end of the clearing.

Suddenly, a burst of gunfire exploded through the air. Chet dropped to the ground. He landed with a thump in a muddy bog and lay face down, still as a corpse, as the fetid water soaked through his T-shirt.

A moment or two of silence passed before a group of boys, all of them about Chet's age, no more than twelve or thirteen, came dashing out of the forest.

Their leader, Marsh Castlebaum, was brandishing a gun, which he pointed at Chet as he rolled his body over with his foot. "He's dead," he declared triumphantly.

"I'm not dead," Chet said, struggling to sit upright.

"You're dead as a doornail," Marsh informed him. "I got you right between the eyes."

Chet swiped his hand across his mud-streaked cheeks and nose. "You just grazed me, man," he said.

Marsh took aim and fired. The cap gun exploded. The acrid smell of burnt gunpowder, and a wispy trail of smoke hung in the air. "You're double dead now. Body-count city."

"That sucks. That really sucks," Chet angrily protested. "You don't know the first thing about war." He jabbed his leg at Marsh and knocked him off-balance into the mud. Marsh grunted and grabbed for Chet's neck with one hand, pounding him on the back with the other. The two boys rolled over and over in the shallow swamp, each struggling to get free of his opponent's grasp.

But before one of them could declare himself the victor, their wrestling match was interrupted by a second bunch of boys, similarly armed with cap guns and rifles, who jumped screaming from the trees into the now-crowded clearing.

Chet and Marsh were instantly allied against their common and far greater enemy. They scrambled to their feet and took off along with the rest of Marsh's soldiers, hotly pursued by the invading forces. In the confusion of battle, it was almost impossible to keep track of who was shooting whom, who had scored a hit, who was dead or wounded.

Stu Simmons felt himself taking one bullet after another as he sprinted after Marsh toward the dirt cliff that rose above the abandoned quarry; the enormous pit, once mined for its gravel, had long since been abandoned by everyone but the town's boys. Its scarred rock faces were striped with red clay dirt. The bottom was filled with water. Stu hurried forward, just as Chet and Marsh jumped off the cliff and rolled down into the dirt. Other boys, still firing and screaming, followed them, each vying to make a more spectacular dive than the one before.

Stu reached the cliff's edge, closed his eyes, and thought about his daddy in Vietnam. His daddy was fighting for America, his mama said. For democracy. He has been there for two years now, and sometimes Stu had to glance at his parents' wedding picture to remember what he looked like.

There was another picture, one that had been taken in Vietnam, which Stu often studied for clues about his father's life as a soldier. He was squinting into the sun, his smiling face unshaven, two fingers held up in the V-for-victory sign. In his other hand, he was holding up his rifle—his M-16, he had written in the accompanying note—and his helmet dangled carelessly from the rifle's bayonet point.

Next to him stood another man, also dressed in camouflage fatigues. "Me and Dodge," his father had written on the back of the photograph. Dodge was his best buddy, his father explained in the note. They watched each other's backs and made sure they didn't get into any bad spots they couldn't get out of. Dodge was from Arkansas, so they spoke the same language. They even liked the same dumb jokes. He hoped that Stu was saving up some of his really dumb ones for him when his tour was up and he finally came home.

Stu closed his eyes and imagined himself sneaking through the jungle, threading a ridge alongside his daddy and Dodge. The Cong were right on their tail, so close by that Stu could hear their guns firing. The situation was bad, but an escape route lay just ahead. Stu knew he had to go first if he was ever going to get the three of them out of this mess.

He let out a deafening cry and hit the ground

running. Holding his breath, he rolled over into a back flip and threw himself over the cliff. He landed in the middle of the quarry a hundred feet below with a force that sent waves of murky green water splashing toward the sky. *Safe,* he thought, swimming toward shore. Wouldn't his daddy have been proud of him today!

CHAPTER ONE

THE TRAIN was leisurely wending its way through western Mississippi, huffing and chugging past the sleepy towns and endless cotton fields and deep, dark forests. Stephen Simmons had already been traveling for a day and a half. But he didn't much mind that the train seemed to stop at each and every country crossroad to let off passengers and take on mail and freight. He was headed for home. He knew he would get there eventually. In the meantime, he was enjoying the ride.

He didn't even mind that the train was hot and stuffy, though he was dressed in full military uniform. After living two years in a steamy Asian jungle, he hardly felt the heat. He was too absorbed in drinking in the scenery that was sliding by his window. He missed these Mississippi fields and trees and sky. Back in Nam, he sometimes dreamed of them and awakened yearning to be back home.

Now, soon, he would be seeing his wife and kids. Looking for work. Getting back to normal. The prospect of settling down to life in Ambertree both thrilled and terrified him. He was used to being a soldier, used to sleeping with his gun for company while jungle bugs buzzed in his ears and mortar fire exploded overhead. He was used to creeping through the swamps and rice paddies, finding the Cong before they found him, protecting himself and his buddies whichever way he had to. He just hoped to God almighty he could get used to being a civilian again.

"Next stop, Ambertree," the conductor announced, ambling through the car. "Five more minutes and you're home, soldier."

Stephen nodded his thanks, adjusted the rim of his cap, and retrieved his duffel bag from the luggage rack. He hoped he looked presentable enough for Lois. He washed his face and shaved a couple of hours ago in the tiny bathroom at the end of the car, nicking his chin as the train lurched around a corner. She would be surprised to see him; until last week, he hadn't known himself when he would be leaving Vietnam.

The train slowed and then came to a stop. "Ambertree!" called out the conductor as Stephen stepped down onto the platform. The station was deserted except for a couple of kids flipping soda-bottle caps onto the tracks. Maybe he should have called ahead to say he was coming. They could have gotten out the high-school band and organized a ticker-tape parade to greet him; Ambertree's very own war hero. He had a chestful of ribbons and medals to prove it.

He looked around and saw that the town was just as run down and poky as when he had left. Across the street, on the ramshackle porch of the general store, five or six old men sat drowsing in the hot afternoon sun. The café next door seemed to be listing toward the ground, weighed down by the kudzu vines growing up its side. The laundromat was a new addition. But the building that housed it was so weather-beaten that one of its gutters tilted crazily from its rusting tin roof.

Home sweet home. Stephen was damn glad to see that nothing much was happening in Ambertree; it was just exactly how he had remembered it.

His house was about a mile's walk from town. By the time he got there, his hand was sweating around the small bouquet of daisies that he had picked along the road. He was hot and thirsty and almost as nervous as he had been his first night out on jungle patrol. He stared at the dilapidated house he had grown up in and shook his head, wondering when it had gotten to be so small. He could already see that the foundation needed shoring up and the paint was peeling badly. Lois had never written him one word about the place being in such a sorry state. He would start fixing it as soon as he had rested up from the trip.

He was halfway up the walk when two kids, a boy and a girl, wandered out of the garage. They were *his* kids, he realized a moment later—Stu and Lidia, his twins, grown so big and tall that he hadn't immediately known them. Feeling strangely shy, he smiled at them and took off his hat. Stu recognized him first and ran flying into his arms. Lidia was right behind him, scrambling down the path and shouting for joy as she threw herself into his embrace.

Their screams brought Lois Simmons hurrying to the front door, where she found her children hanging from her husband's arms. It took her a moment to understand that she wasn't dreaming, that this was truly Stephen, standing there in front of her. He pressed her close to him, and she was inhaling his familiar, comforting smell. "Thank the Lord, you're safe," she murmured, laughing and crying against his shoulder. "Thank the Lord, you're home to stay."

Lidia had been keeping a diary since the end of fifth grade. Her goal was to write at least two entries a week, though she didn't always have the time because of her homework and having to help her mother around the house. She confided in her diary her most secret, private thoughts: which boy she was in love with, what she wanted to be when she grew up, how it felt to be twelve years old and Stu's twin.

She was younger than Stu by only three minutes. He loved to tell people that the minute he got born, he turned around to look at his accomplishment—and there was Lidia's head, following right behind him. "I've been tryin' to lose her ever since," he always said. "And so far, he's failed," Lidia always reminded him.

Some folks had trouble believing they were twins, because they didn't much resemble each other. Stu was big for his age, already developing muscles like his father's. He had blond hair and pale green eyes, and an impish grin that seemed to make people feel good.

Her mamma always said she would grow into

being pretty, but Lidia only had to look in the mirror to know she had gotten shortchanged.

"That Lidia's such a skinny little thing," she had overheard a lady whisper at the grocery story. "Ain't it a shame that the boy got all the looks!"

However, what she lacked in appearance, she made up for in brains. Stu might be older, but she was smarter, and together they made a good team. Usually, her diary was full of stories about whatever mischief they had been up to. But in the days after her daddy came back from the war, Lidia wrote very little about herself or Stu. She had too much to say about what her daddy was going through, and most of it wasn't good.

She was so tickled to have him home that she didn't care if he woke them all up night after night with his screaming. Mamma explained that Daddy was having bad nightmares, on account of remembering the terrible things he had seen in Vietnam.

"Dear Diary," Lidia wrote after he had been home a week, "I sure do wish I could ask Daddy what them dreams are about, 'cause I am real curious what could make him yell and carry on like he does. But mamma said to leave him be and let him get on with forgetting the bad stuff he left behind."

The situation got more curious still, when one day, just before suppertime, a man drove up to their house in a shiny black Cadillac. Lidia and Stu wanted to run outside to see the car up close, but Mamma said, "No, y'all stay put and let your daddy handle this."

They watched from the window as their father went out to speak to the man. "What's he want?" Lidia asked her mamma.

It didn't take much imagination to figure out that her father wasn't pleased with whatever the man was saying. Daddy was shaking his head and getting red in the face and sticking his fist under the man's nose. The man backed away, but not quickly enough, because Daddy stepped forward and gave the Cadillac a swift, hard kick.

"Isn't he from the bank, Mamma?" said Stu. The man jerked open his car door, got in, and drove away. "What's he and Daddy quarrelin' about?"

Her mother shook her head and shooed them away from the window. "Never mind," she said, her lips tightening. "And don't be asking your daddy a whole lot of questions. He's got enough to worry about without you two bothering him."

Her father's nightmares must have been especially terrible that night. He woke up yelling again, and before Mamma could stop him, he rushed out of the house and climbed onto the roof. He kept on shouting so loudly Lidia was sure the whole neighborhood must be awake and listening.

Lidia and Stu stood on the grass in their pajamas while their mother begged him to please hush and come on down where she could talk to him. But Daddy seemed not to hear her. He was crouched on the roof, pointing his finger as if it were a gun, screaming at some terrible thing in the distance that no one else could see.

One of the neighbors must have called the

police, because just then a police car zoomed up the street and stopped at their house. Its siren shrieked and its red and blue lights flashed in the darkness, adding to the excitement. Before long, two more police cars had pulled up. The policemen hurriedly conferred; then began climbing up the side of the house to the roof, all the while urging Stephen Simmons to get down before he hurt himself.

"No! You can't take me!" he howled, sounding so much like an animal in pain that Lidia wanted to run inside and cover her ears with her pillow to keep from hearing him. But her feet wouldn't move; she felt stuck to the spot, as if forced to watch a terrifying movie in which her father was playing the starring role.

"No!" he screamed again as the cops advanced toward him on the roof. Stu grabbed for her hand. They clutched at each other for comfort as their father thrust out his arms and legs karate-style. He knocked down the first two cops; then four more came after him, waving their nightsticks and threatening to knock him down. After several moments, they managed to subdue him and wrestle him off the roof.

"We got to help him," said Stu, and they rushed to pull him away from the cops.

They didn't have a chance. It was six cops to two kids, and the fight was over before it began. With his hands cuffed behind him, Stephen Simmons was thrown into the back of a squad car and hauled off to jail.

"On a charge of disturbing the peace," one of the

officers told Lois. "I don't care what kind of war hero he is. He can't be keeping folks from sleeping. Besides, he's a danger to himself. Your husband needs help."

Their father had been gone a week—looking for work, their mamma told them—when a deputy sheriff knocked on their door and handed Lois Simmons something he called a court order. The house was declared unfit to be lived in. They had twenty-four hours to remove their belongings and get out before the bulldozer came to flatten the house to the ground.

"Says who?" Lidia asked the deputy sheriff. She imagined the bulldozer with the face of the big, bad wolf, huffing and puffing to blow their house down.

"Hush," her mamma said. "The man's just doing his job. They could have kicked us out of here long ago, except that your daddy was gone."

As far as Lidia could see, her daddy was still gone, and twenty-four hours were nowhere near enough time to clear out a lifetime of cherished possessions. But since the night the police had hauled her daddy away in handcuffs, like he was a thief or a murderer, she discovered that it was easier to go numb, to feel nothing rather than to try to make sense of what was happening.

She wondered what Stu was thinking as they trudged in and out of the house, hauling their clothes and toys, and helping Mamma drag the few pieces of furniture that could fit into the house trailer where they were moving. Usually— most likely because they were twins—Lidia knew what Stu was feeling just by looking at his face. Sometimes, she felt as if she could even read his mind.

But today, whatever he was feeling was hidden from her. It was spooky how nothing showed in his eyes, except for an occasional flicker of anger when she caught him staring at the sign in front of the house that said in great big bold letters, "This house condemned."

Their pickup truck was already filled to bursting when the bulldozer arrived. The driver circled their house, moving ever closer, as if to hurry them along.

"Let's go, kids," Lois called, wanting to be gone before the bulldozer began destroying their house and everything they had to leave behind.

Lidia walked slowly to the truck, climbed inside, and stared out the window to get a last look at her home. There was her brother, dragging their father's army footlocker out of the garage and across the grass just as the bulldozer struck, collapsing the front of the house.

Lidia watched in horror as one wall after another crumpled into chunks of plaster dust. Their entire life was being laid bare, their most private secrets exposed to any curious onlooker. She reached down to help Stu lift himself and the locker onto the seat next to her. When she looked again at the house, she could hardly keep from crying.

The Lipnicki kids had descended like a band of vultures. She had always hated those damn Lipnickis, but never more than now as they picked through the rubble, scavenging for any item of value left behind.

She and Stu stared at each other. This time she had no trouble reading his thoughts. She grabbed his hand and they nodded in silent agreement. The Lipnickis were the neighborhood bullies. She didn't know how or when, but some day soon, she and Stu would make them pay for what they were doing.

CHAPTER TWO

SOME DAYS Stu wished he were any place else on earth but Ambertree. He hated the cramped little trailer that was now his family's home. He hated that his mother never seemed to smile anymore, no matter how he tried to cheer her up. Some days his life was so filled up with doing chores and keeping Lidia out of mischief that he felt as if he didn't have room enough to think. It was tough work being the man of the house. He had waited so long for his daddy to return from Vietnam; now he was gone again, and no one had the least idea when he would be back.

If his father were home, Stu wouldn't have been on his way to town with Lidia and their friend, Elvadine. They would be out together fishing or hunting for rabbit or maybe even taking a swim. Instead, he was stuck here, bouncing up and down in the front seat of the truck, the broken springs poking into his behind every time the wheels hit a pothole, where the tar had melted and cracked under the blazing summer sun.

They passed a Coca-Cola sign and Stu sighed. He imagined himself gulping down a cold Coke, dangling his fishing line in the water. "Lidia," he said, trying to wheedle her, "you think maybe you could do the laundry without me, this one time?"

"No," said Lidia, who was hunched in the driver's seat, one hand on the wheel, the other beating time to the rock 'n' roll music blasting on the radio. She took a long drag on her cigarette and exhaled a cloud of smoke, which Stu waved away impatiently. He stared out the window, sulking, using his silence to punish Lidia.

Lidia knew Stu was paying her back for being the boss. Pointedly ignoring him, she slid open the window that separated the cab from the back of the truck and called to Elvadine, "How you doing back there? Getting everything separated?"

Elvadine was crawling on her hands and knees, surrounded by five huge bags of dirty clothes that she was struggling to divide into piles by color. "'Separate a few things for me back there, would you, Elvadine?'" she petulantly mimicked Lidia's earlier request. "Next time you say I ain't a good friend to you, I'm gonna slap your face!"

Elvadine and Lidia were like Laurel and Hardy, so oddly paired that people shook their heads to see them together. Elvadine was black and talked with a thick country accent that the boys at school loved to mock. Her hair was a kinky tangle of curls that couldn't be tamed by any amount of grease, and she was as deliberate and slow to move as Lidia was impulsive and restless.

But Lidia never minded people's mocking stares or laughter. Elvadine had been her best friend since they were little girls, and Lidia knew she could always count on her for three things: she would follow Lidia to the ends of the earth; she would do whatever Lidia asked of her; and she would complain about it every step of the way.

Elvadine's threats were nothing but hot air, and they both knew it. Lidia tossed her cigarette out the window and sang along with the radio.

"Hell, Lidia. Twelve dang years old and smokin'," Stu said, paying her back for insisting he do women's work.

"I can't help it," she defended herself. "I'm an addict."

"How many of them you smoke a week?"

She shrugged. "I don't know. Two."

"Smokin' two cigarettes a week don't make you no addict. It just makes you an idiot," he scolded.

Lidia didn't even bother answering him. She slowed down as they approached the town limits. Just ahead of them, without any warning, a car pulled out of a parking lot. The driver cut them off, forcing Lidia to slam on the brakes to avoid being sideswiped. Elvadine got the worst of it, smashing into the back window. "Don't be clamping on them brakes. You near about busted my head," she shrieked, rubbing her temple.

Lidia leaned on her horn. It didn't make a lick of sense that she couldn't get a license because she was a kid, yet she was a better driver than half the people on the road. "Jesus H. Christ! What the hell's this cheeseball think he's doing?"

"Well, if you wouldn't tailgate," Stu said. "You follow people closer than bark on a tree."

"He made me miss the street!" she said indignantly.

"Well, turn around!"

The brakes squealed again as she made a U-turn in the middle of the street, almost crashing into the car behind her. The outraged driver blasted his horn at her, and Elvadine screamed. "I know you're trying to kill me! Make way, I'm coming in," she said, trying to crawl through the window into the cab.

"Ah, Jesus!" Stu sputtered. He was better off walking the rest of the way to the laundromat instead of spending another second in the truck. "Pull over, I'm getting out."

"Don't look now, but I smell bacon," Elvadine said suddenly.

Stu glanced in the rearview mirror. "Ah, hell, Lidia! There's a damn cop! There go his lights!"

Lidia slammed her foot on the gas, turned right at the corner, and careened down the street. The cop was right behind them, his siren blaring. Elvadine screeched, and Stu tightened his seat belt. If Lidia didn't wrap the truck around a tree, they were going to end up in jail, for sure.

"You trying to get us arrested?" he yelled as she floored the gas.

"No! Why do you think I'm running from him? Climb in, Elvadine!"

"I can't! I'm stuck!" she wailed, still struggling to wriggle her way into the cab. "That policeman gonna come up with his gun drawn and he gonna shoot me in the butt."

Lidia whipped around another corner. "Don't just sit there!" she hissed at Stu. "Help her!"

"You deaf? She said she's stuck!"

"I know that, dummy. Unstick her!"

Stu grabbed Elvadine under the armpits and grunted as he struggled to pry her free.

"What are you doin' with your hands?" she whined.

"I'm *trying* to free you." He felt as if he were wrestling with a stuck pig—except that pigs didn't talk back. Whereas Elvadine, instead of thanking him for his help, was cursing him and saying, "Don't you get too free with your hands now, boy."

"I ain't doing this 'cause I like it," he informed her, pulling as hard as he could. She screamed as the truck hit a bump, which sent her tumbling head first into the cab, landing between Lidia and Stu.

"You're on the gear shift!" Lidia complained.

Elvadine moaned and rubbed the spot on her thigh that had taken the brunt of her fall. "I think I know that!" she said, moving away from the shift.

Stu clutched at the dashboard and mouthed a silent string of curses. These damn fool girls were driving him nuts. He wasn't ever going anywhere again with his sister at the wheel. He should have jumped out when he still had a chance to make it to town in one piece. He checked the rear view again and watched the squad car speed up behind them. "Slow down so he don't throw us in jail for resisting arrest," he said.

Finally, Lidia listened to him and removed her foot from the gas pedal. But to their amazement, the squad car kept going; it zoomed past them, obviously intent on capturing some other, more dangerous menace to society, further down the road.

Lidia heaved a sigh of relief; her family couldn't afford the least bit more shame or dishonor just now. What would her mamma say if she'd had to collect her kids from the police station? She brought the truck to a sedate halt in front of the courthouse and slumped in her seat. "Well, what do you know? He was after someone else," she mumbled, feeling the sweat trickling down her bikini top.

"I think I just lost my virginity," Elvadine said dolefully.

Stu glared at them. "I'm outta here!" he said. He hopped out of the cab and slammed the door.

"Where you goin'?" Lidia demanded.

"Elvis has left the building!" he yelled over his shoulder and angrily stalked away.

"It seem to you like he be mad about somethin'?" Elvadine asked in her most deadpan voice.

Lidia giggled. "I guess he never touched a girl before," she cracked, and both of them began to laugh so hard that Lidia got the hiccups and they almost wet their pants.

It took a while before they calmed down enough to dump the laundry bags out of the truck. Then Lidia hiccuped, and they doubled over, giggling again as they dragged the bags along the sidewalk to the laundromat. They were halfway there, when horrible Lester Lucket sauntered out of the dime store and caught sight of them.

Lester had teased them all year long at school.

Now, his face lit up with glee as he hooked his thumbs in his jeans' pockets and blocked their path. "Well, if it ain't frog-face and nigger-butt," he said.

Lidia bristled at his insults. Then she remembered what her mamma had said about keeping out of trouble. Though the words trembled on her lips, she held back from telling him he had the ugliest face in two counties and the I.Q. of an ass, and said only, "Shut up, Lester."

"Make me," he challenged, taking a step closer and sticking out his chest.

His bad breath floated across the space between them. She bet he hadn't brushed his teeth in a month. "I make you every morning," she shot back.

"'Cuz you hang out with that fat jiggaboo."

Lidia could feel Elvadine beside her trembling with anger. "Don't you say that to her!" she yelled, balling her fists.

"I'll say what I like." Lester sneered and pointed a dirty index finger at Elvadine. "Fat nigger!" He raised his hand to swing at Elvadine, but Lidia was too fast for him. She scooped up a rock, hurled it at his face, and hit him square in the mouth.

He screamed and spat a gush of blood as one of his front teeth dropped into his palm.

"You call us names like that again," Lidia said, "I'll knock out all your teeth!"

Lester pressed his hand to his mouth. "I'm gonna get you for this! I swear I am!" he said, scrambling to put distance between them.

Lidia shook her head as she watched him

scurry down the street. "I swear to God, he makes me so mad. Where does he get off, calling you names like that?"

"At the rate that boy's going, he's gonna be toothless and brain dead. Ain't that the second tooth you knocked out of his head this month?"

The image of Lester flapping his lips around toothless gums like an old man made Elvadine burst into laughter, which naturally got Lidia going again. They were still giggling and poking each other, and didn't notice Lois Simmons come out of the Dairy Queen and cross the street.

But when they looked up, there she was, in front of them, frowning at Lidia. "How many times have I told you not to go beating up on boys?" she said sternly. She put one hand under Lidia's chin, forcing her daughter to meet her gaze.

Lidia blushed with shame. She had promised to be a good girl, and now she disappointed her mother by beating Lester up; but she couldn't let him get away with mocking them or punching Elvadine. Lester had declared war on them. Why didn't her mother understand that she'd had no other choice but to hit him?

Stu couldn't stop thinking about the old Coca-Cola sign, calling to him from the side of the building. "Drink Coca-Cola," it said. "Thirst knows no season." Well, this was summer, and he surely was thirsty.

He passed the sign a second time, on his way out of town after he had ditched the girls. Later, there would be hell to pay, with Lidia carrying on because he left them with all those bags of laundry. But he didn't care. He needed to be alone, away from their yakking and giggling, away from Lidia forever telling him what to do.

He thought about calling on his friends to see if they wanted to go for a swim and catch some fish. But something held him back, and instead he started walking with no particular destination in mind. His feet kept on going, leading him down a road he knew so well he could have walked it in his sleep, until eventually he found himself walking up the path to his house—at least, what had once been his house. He hadn't seen it since the day they knocked it down, and now he almost wished he hadn't come back. He didn't know which was worse: the "Condemned" sign near the road or the pile of shattered concrete, splintered glass, and tiles that the bulldozer had left behind, sad souvenirs of his family's history. Even the mailbox was broken into pieces, though Stu suspected it was the Lipnickis' doing, not the bulldozer's.

Someone had yanked the toilet off its base in what had once been the bathroom, and turned it upside down. Stu righted it and sat down on the bowl to contemplate the ruins of his life. A family of sparrows twittered in the old oak trees that stood in the nearby corn field. Otherwise, there was silence.

The air felt close around him, the heat oppressive. He was thirsty and tired. He lay on a thick green lawn, shaded by the drooping branches of a magnolia tree and lost himself in a daydream: behind him was his family's house; it was two stories high and freshly painted; the door opened and his mother came out onto the porch; she called to him, asking did he want a Coke from the refrigerator and some of the brownies she had just taken out of the oven.

Stu smacked his lips, almost able to taste those brownies and that icy cold Coke. He wondered whether he could imagine his thirst away if he tried hard enough. He shut his eyes and thought about a long gulp of Coke streaming into his mouth and down his throat.

His fantasy was suddenly interrupted by the sound of a car pulling up, followed by a loud honking. "Go away, Lidia!" he yelled.

The car door slammed, and he heard the sound of footsteps coming toward him. *Damn,* he thought. That girl couldn't leave him be, not even for an hour. "Lidia," he sighed, "I told you, get lost—"

But his irritation vanished as the intruder walked into his field of vision. "Daddy!" he cried, leaping up and tearing across the field to hug his father. "You're back! When did you get back?"

"Well, I guess just now," Stephen Simmons said. He smiled at his son as if he had just been handed a million dollars, and ruffled his hair. Then he turned to gaze at the empty lot. "Lookit, here," he said quietly.

The lump that had been lodged in Stu's throat since the house had been razed began to dissolve.

"They took our house away," he said, blinking back the tears that boys weren't allowed to shed.

Stephen let out a low whistle. "They sure did. A monument to architectural history, that's what she was. Just give me one good reason why they had to plow her down."

"Termites." Stu repeated his mother's explanation.

"Character, that's what she had. I bet it took 'em all day to bring her to her knees, didn't it?"

"I think she just fell down on her own as soon as she seen the bulldozer comin'," Stu said.

Stephen shaded his eyes and looked at the wreckage. "We sure had ourselves a lot of good times in this old place, didn't we?"

Stu nodded. The heavy load of responsibility he had been carrying already felt lighter.

"Yeah," Stephen went on. "Well, we're gonna have to get ourselves a new home of our own."

"You got a job," Stu said excitedly. "I knew it!"

Stephen shook his head. "Not yet, son, but I will." He picked up a chunk of concrete and closed his fist around it. Then he asked, "Did your mamma tell you about where I been all this time?"

"Lookin' for work."

"Well, I suspect she didn't wanna say where I really was. I been sick. That night them policemen came? They took me to a hospital."

"For what?"

"Well, I went nuts for a little while," Stephen said. "Bein' in the war. I still have nightmares about it."

Stu watched a gray squirrel scurry across the grass a few feet away from them. Bad dreams about the war. . . . So that explained his father's screams in the night. But now he seemed like his regular old self—he wasn't acting or sounding crazy— so the doctors must have fixed him up just fine.

Stu was glad that his daddy knew he could be trusted with this secret, and especially that he was hearing it before Lidia did. "Can I see your scar again?" he asked.

"Most of my scars are in my head," said Stephen.

"No, I mean the one on your stomach."

Stephen obligingly pulled up his shirt, revealing a thick red scar that ran from his breast to just above his belly button.

Stu had seen the scar before, but it never failed to impress him. "That is the most disgusting zipper I ever seen," he said approvingly.

"Glad you enjoyed it."

"Tell me about the fightin' and all," Stu urged. "Tell me about being a hero."

Stephen hesitated a moment, sensing how much his son wanted to prolong this time alone with him. But they would have plenty of other days, and he was eager to see the rest of the family. "Another day," he promised Stu. "I suspect we ought to be gettin' on home. I ain't seen your mom or your sister yet."

"Dad?" said Stu.

"Yeah?"

"You're back for good now, aren't you?"

Stephen slung his arm around Stu's shoulder and nodded. "I'm back for good," he said.

"How much will the books cost?" asked Lois, cradling the telephone receiver under her ear so her hands were free to rinse out the soda bottles she had lined up by the sink. She grimaced at the answer. "I'll get back to you real soon," she said to the person at the other end.

Lidia stood next to her at the sink, peeling potatoes for dinner. "That's why you been collecting all those bottles, to go out and ruin your life by voluntarily taking classes?" she said, after Lois had hung up the phone.

Lois smiled. "If I can take one business class, they'll let me manage the Dixie Queen and pay me twice as much money as I make now." Though, considering how expensive the books were, she would be hunting for bottles a whole lot longer than she had planned.

Money; she worried about it early in the morning when she first woke up and late at night, when she couldn't sleep because she was figuring out how to pay the bills. If only Stephen were home and working, they could start to catch up, pay off some of their debts. If only she had someone to turn to, someone who would give her the money for school. If only—.

Stop it, she told herself. "If only" never paid the rent or put food on the table. They managed okay up until now, and she just had to keep on believing everything would turn out all right.

Her more immediate concern was Stu, who

should have been home long ago. Hoping to see him walking down the road, she glanced out the window and almost dropped the bottle in her hand. "Lidia," she said, almost choking on the words, "you better set another place at the table."

The quaver in her voice caught Lidia's attention and brought her instantly to the window. "Daddy!" she shouted, racing out the door and into his arms.

Lois hurriedly stacked the soda bottles out of sight, under the kitchen cabinet, and followed Lidia onto the porch to welcome Stephen home. Her heart singing, she watched him cover the few yards between them. Lord, he was handsome! She loved him since junior high school, and she didn't think she could ever stop loving him. They'd had their troubles, as any married couple did, but his shy smile and slow-talking way still made her feel young and innocent.

"Miss me?" he asked her, stepping onto the porch and reaching out a hand.

She smiled and thought her face might break in two. "Hell, no," she lied and fell into his arms. There was no way she would let him go, not ever again. This time, he was staying home for good.

CHAPTER THREE

THE SUN was rising over Ambertree. A freight train chugged through town, heading north to Grenada. The conductor hooted his whistle as he passed the shanty town, once occupied by impoverished cotton-mill workers and their families. The mill had long since closed, and most of the workers had moved on, abandoning their rickety shacks to down-on-their-luck locals, like the Simmonses, who couldn't afford to live anywhere else.

Jimmy Owen, the Simmons' next-door neighbor, was sprawled on his stoop, drinking cheap wine straight out of the jug. From the kitchen window, Lidia watched him cough up a glob of evil-looking yellow phlegm and light another hand-rolled cigarette.

Her mamma called Jimmy a sad case. He was usually drunk by the time most people were sitting down to breakfast, and he said rude words to Lidia and Elvadine. But at least he minded his own business, unlike Mrs. Higgens, the nosy old busybody who was standing at her door, her head all done up in pincurls, pretending to shake out her rug while she surveyed the street.

"Simmons!" she screamed. "Your house is on fire again!"

Lidia stuck out her tongue as Mrs. Higgens shook her head and went back inside. The old witch kept threatening to call the fire department because of all the smoke that billowed out the window whenever Lidia did the cooking.

This morning, because Lois was late for work at the Dixie Queen, Lidia was in charge, frying up a pan of eggs and Spam. Her mother was already dressed in her starched white uniform, with her hair pulled back in a tight ponytail. Lidia thought it must be fun to work in a restaurant, calling out the orders and talking to the customers. Pretending she was the Dixie Queen cook, she flipped the eggs and Spam, which were deliciously sizzling in a thick layer of grease. The eggs were cooking just the way she liked them—well-done and black around the edges.

Stu stumbled into the room, still groggy with sleep. He poked at the charred bread that stuck out of the toaster, made a face at the frying pan, and went to the cupboard to pull out a box of Lucky Charms cereal.

"I'm cooking breakfast," said Lidia, feeling unappreciated.

Stu poured cereal into a bowl. "That's why I'm eatin' Lucky Charms."

"We can't waste food, son," Lois told him. "You need to eat what your sister's making."

Stu considered the sputtering black mess in the frying pan. "She's making soot," he said. But rather than get into a fight, he poured the cereal back in the box and put it back on the shelf. He cheered up as his father came in and sat down at the table. "How'd you sleep, Dad?" he asked, sitting down next to him.

"Just fine, thanks," Stephen said, smiling at Lois.

Stu sighed gratefully. Fine meant no nightmares and no going back to the hospital.

"What are your plans for this morning?" Stephen asked him.

Stu leaned in close and lowered his voice so Lidia wouldn't hear him. "Me and the guys are going to build a fort by the big old Thunder Oak you once showed me past Conner's Ridge."

"That sounds like a great idea," whispered Stephen.

"Okay, everything's cooked well enough," Lidia announced. "I guess I'm near done." She sat down, and Lois dished out helpings to everyone.

"Mmm . . . eggs and everything. And look how nice it all goes together," Stephen said, his eyes twinkling as he glanced at his wife.

"Dad, since this is your first morning home, would you like to have my bacon?" Lidia offered.

Stephen worked hard to suppress a grin. He said, "That's nice, Pumpkin, but you go ahead and eat it."

"Gee, Lidia," Stu said, holding up a rectangular object, burned beyond crisp, that once had been a piece of bread. "Maybe you ought to cook this some more. I can still tell what it is."

His father put his much larger hand over Stu's

and silenced him with a look. "Stu, you want to do us the honor of sayin' grace?" he said firmly.

Stu obediently folded his hands under his chin. "Dear Lord, bless this food," he said, eyeing his plate. "Please."

As soon as breakfast was over and the dishes were done, Stu hurried off to the woods to rendezvous with his pals. Chet and Marsh were dressed for action. A radio in the shape of a hand grenade dangled around Marsh's neck, and Chet had a pair of binoculars tied to his belt. They both brought their bikes, on which were balanced cardboard boxes filled with scraps of wood, odd pieces of plastic, and other junk they had collected for their fort.

Stu arrived empty-handed, so he felt responsible for digging up more material along the way. But the pickings were pretty slim. "Anybody want another piece of rotted wood with dead bugs stuck to it?" he joked, raising the top of a dumpster and examining its contents.

"Screw that, man. So whose house we goin' to first to get some good stuff?" said Marsh, who had a hot-tempered, rebellious streak that frequently landed him and his friends in trouble.

"My dad says if I hawk anything off of our property, he'll use my butt for fish bait," Chet said dolefully.

"Don't look at me," said Stu. "All our stuff got hauled away."

With his foot, Marsh took aim at a tin can and sent it spinning into the trees. "Well, that's just great! So we're supposed to build this fort out of cardboard? I doubt it! Let's go to the quarry. We'll find something there."

"The Lipnickis claim the quarry," said Chet, trying as usual to rein in Marsh.

"So?" said Stu, who welcomed the opportunity to take on the Lipnickis.

"You're such a wimp, Chet," Marsh jeered. "We're gonna avoid them all summer again? What are we, the pussy posse?"

Two against one; Chet could either walk away from the challenge and never hear the end of it or hope his buddies knew what they were doing. "Fine. Let's go," he said. "So your dad's back, huh?" he asked Stu as they circled the barbed wire fence that surrounded the quarry.

Stu nodded. "Yeah. For good this time."

"Cool. Where's he been?"

"Uh . . . looking for work," Stu stammered. No way he could tell the truth to anyone, not even Chet, his best friend. Fortunately for him, they just reached the spot where there was a gap between the barbed wire and the ground wide enough for them to scramble underneath the fence.

"Well, lookit here!" Chet declared gleefully. He pointed to the mound of corrugated metal, rusted girders, and old timber that over the years had been dumped in the quarry. It was exactly what they needed for their fort.

"Let's go. Maybe we can haul some of that stuff outta here," said Stu. But as they began their descent into the pit, a chorus of war cries pierced the air.

On the far end of the quarry, the two oldest Lipnickis—Arliss, who was fifteen, and Leo, who was a year younger—were taking turns jumping off the rocks into the water.

"Told you they'd be here," Chet said nervously. "Let's get out of here."

"Hold up. I wanna see this. They're playin' suicide," Marsh said.

They watched as Leo dived from the side of the quarry wall into the shallow pool thirty feet below. A spray of water shot up around him as he sank beneath the surface; he reappeared a moment later, his fist raised in exultation. Next, Arliss took a turn. He launched himself from an even higher point on the cliff, somersaulted in midfall, and belly flopped onto the water.

"Are they nuts or are they nuts?" hooted Marsh.

"You tryin' to talk about my family?"

The boys whirled around and found themselves face-to-face with Ula, the thirteen-year-old Lipnicki, who already towered over most of the boys in her class. She was wearing a stained sundress, and thongs on her feet that badly needed washing. Her hair was long and stringy and looked as if it, too, hadn't been washed in some time.

Stu stared at her with a mixture of fear and fascination. Even he could see that beneath the grime and sullen expression was a pretty face. "Hey there, Ula. How's life treatin' you today?" he said, in his friendliest voice.

"Don't talk to me!" Ula snapped. "Don't look at

me, neither." She cupped her hands to her mouth and shouted, "Arliss! Leo! Caught me some trespassers over here!"

"Well." Marsh smiled weakly. "Nice speaking with you." He edged away from her, followed by Stu and Chet. But Ula was too fast for them. She grabbed a thick branch and swung it at them.

"We're toast," Chet muttered to Stu.

"Maybe not. There's only three of 'em. Figure you can take the big guy?" Stu whispered.

Chet gulped. "Oh, sure."

"Honestly?"

"No."

"What about the little guy?"

"No."

"The girl?" Stu asked hopefully.

Chet hesitated a moment, then came up with the truth. "No."

"Saying you wanna run?"

"Yep."

But it was too late. Three more of the Lipnicki clan—Willard, who was twelve and a half; Darla, who was their age; and Ebb, who was ten—had moved in behind them as stealthily as deer hunters coming in for the kill; then came Arliss and Leo, who had climbed down from the cliff to join them alongside Ula.

They were a fearsome bunch—tough and mean and always spoiling for a fight. Stu had tangled with a couple of them years before. Since then, his policy was to avoid them as much as possible; now he and his friends had stupidly managed to get cornered by the whole lot of them, a lynch mob about to pounce.

He surreptitiously eyed the ground for a weapon, but saw nothing within reach he could use to defend himself. Besides, they were outnumbered, two to one, and the Lipnickis took no prisoners. He took a deep breath and tried to imagine what his father would have done when he found himself outnumbered by the enemy. *Stay calm and stand tough,* he thought. This was war, a fight for honor and survival.

Arliss made the first move. He grabbed Marsh by the front of his shirt and spun him around like a top. He slammed one arm around him in a body lock and clamped his free hand over Marsh's eyes. Willard and Ebb immediately stepped forward to block Stu and Chet from helping their friend.

"Ow!" Marsh groaned, blind and helpless in Arliss' grasp.

"You got some nerve, trespasser, slinkin' on to our territory, speakin' ill of us," Arliss berated him.

"Not me, man," Marsh whined, trying to wriggle free. "I was just sayin' how brave y'all were."

Arliss scowled. He shoved Marsh forward so his head hung between his legs. Then he kneed him in the butt. "You better quit lyin'!" he said, as Marsh groaned again, sounding as if he were in real pain.

"Why don't you just let him go? Pick on somebody your own size," Stu said, surprising himself.

"Maybe you got a point." Arliss seemed to consider Stu's suggestion. Then he nodded. "Ebb?"

Ebb responded so quickly that Stu realized only after he hit the ground that he had been kicked in the face. He was dizzy from the blow, but he forced himself upright and raised his fists to strike back. Ebb got him in the chest this time and knocked him to the ground. Again, Stu managed to struggle to his feet. He blinked, looking for Ebb, but he was so disoriented that he couldn't find his foe until Chet pointed him in the right direction.

Before he could throw even one punch, Ebb clobbered him in the gut. He doubled over with pain. Ebb hammered mercilessly at his neck until he knocked Stu backwards and laid him out flat on his back. Stu gasped for breath and rolled over to save his face and stomach from more punishment. He was beyond trying to fight back; he had been beaten—the taste of blood was in his mouth.

"Hey, you kids!" A man's voice rang out above the Lipnickis' cheers. "What's going on?"

Stu raised himself to his elbow and saw a tall, broad-shouldered man standing near the dumpsters, a few yards away. The Lipnickis saw him, too. They must have realized he wasn't someone to tangle with, because Arliss suddenly let go of Marsh.

"Nothin's going on," Arliss answered the man. "He just fell."

"Better get your butts out of here before the cops get wind of you all," the man warned them.

Chet was all set to take his advice. "C'mon, man," he said, helping Stu stand up. "Let's get out of here. Marsh?"

But Arliss had a few parting words for Marsh.

"Quarry's ours," he crowed. "You better don't come back, 'less you wanna leave in an ambulance!"

"Pick a finger!" Marsh growled. Emboldened by their protector's watchful presence, he held up one hand and wagged his index finger under Arliss' nose.

Chet and Stu grabbed his arms and pulled him away while the Lipnickis slinked off in the opposite direction.

"You okay?" Chet asked.

Stu nodded and wiped the blood from his nose and lip; he still felt dizzy, but he was okay.

"You were a crazy man back there," said Chet. "I'm proud of you."

"Did I hit him?"

"No, but you sure impressed us all with your tenacity," Chet assured him.

Marsh stalked ahead, venting his anger by trampling the flowers that bordered the path. Finally, he burst out, "One of us ought to go back there and kick some ass!"

Stu and Chet exchanged knowing glances. This morning's encounter was one more example of Marsh's rashness.

"I agree," said Chet.

"Me, too," said Stu solemnly.

"You have our full support," Chet said.

"I'm serious, you guys!" Marsh insisted. "We could make us some Molotov cocktails and na-palm them bastards."

Another look passed between his friends. Marsh was big on talk, short on action. Molotov cocktails? Marsh couldn't even make his own peanut butter and jelly sandwiches.

"Forget it, Marsh. They're jerks," Chet said. "Doesn't mean we gotta fight 'em."

Stu shook his head. He'd had enough fighting for one day, and he knew that Marsh was just blowing off steam because the Lipnickis had humiliated him. But he disagreed with Chet about one thing. He would have to do battle against them again; it was a matter of pride. "We'll get them. When the time is right, we'll get them," he promised.

"Sure, Stu," said Chet. "But right now, we're gonna build us the coolest fort ever. Just gonna be ours, man."

But the excitement had leaked out of their plan, like air from a punctured balloon.

"Yeah, cool," Marsh said disconsolately.

Stu turned to stare at the Lipnickis, who were ambling up the hill toward home. He remembered something his father had told him a long time ago, before he had gone off to 'Nam: A man could lose a battle and still win the war. Oh yes, when the right moment came, his revenge would be sweet.

Lidia stood on Elvadine's shoulders to boost herself over the fence that surrounded the old cotton mill. The mill had been shut down years earlier, but the fence remained, as had John Lipnicki, the former night security guard. After the closing, John occupied the foreman's shack. He had thwarted all of the owners' legal maneuvers to evict him. Eventually, they gave up, leaving John to live there with his family in splendid isolation.

He made ends meet by scrounging for junk which he sold for a few pennies, as the need arose. His yard could easily have passed for the town dump. It drew Lidia like a magnet, moving her to ignore the risks involved in messing with the Lipnickis.

She knew all about Stu's fort. She had been eavesdropping on him and his friends, listening to their plans, creating her own schemes to surprise them. To help her out, she enlisted Elvadine, along with Elvadine's cousin, Amber.

Naturally, Elvadine said flat out she was nuts. Boys built forts; girls went calling on them after the dirty work was done, particularly when building the fort meant stealing from the Lipnickis. But in the end, because she couldn't say no to Lidia, Elvadine joined her expedition.

Elvadine was still fretting as Lidia vaulted over the fence and picked up the board she had spied from the other side. "If those crazy Lipnickis catch us, we're deader than dog meat," she grumbled. "Let's get out of here."

Lidia tossed the board to Amber, who threw it into her wagon. "I only got three boards," said Lidia, looking around for more.

"Well, that's three more than you had five minutes ago. I'm not stayin' one more minute. Let's go, Amber," Elvadine beckoned to her cousin.

Lidia stared at them in disgust. Some friends they were, not to stick around and wait for her.

They were wimps and cowards, both of them. She scrambled up the fence and hauled herself over, pleased that she could manage it alone. Then she hustled to catch up with them, yelling, "They got everything you could imagine back there."

Elvadine could not have cared less. Every time Lidia's head got filled up with another of her damn fool notions, Elvadine had to straighten things out. Thank you very much, but she wanted nothing to do with the Lipnickis.

Much as she loved Lidia, Elvadine wished that the good Lord had handed her a bigger dose of plain old common sense. The girl just didn't know when to stop. One of these days, she was going to outsmart herself and go prancing too far over the edge of disaster. Elvadine swore that she wasn't going to be the one to haul her back up from the pit.

To get rid of these dark thoughts, she turned on her transistor radio and fiddled with the dial until she hit on one of her favorite songs by the Supremes. She grinned at Amber. They had worked out a dance routine that matched the words and beat. She figured they were as good as any of the groups they saw on "American Bandstand." Maybe if they kept on practicing, one day they would have a shot at getting on TV themselves.

Now, they snapped their fingers, clapped their hands, and danced the steps they had practiced so often. They sang along with the radio:
"I wake up in the morning,
And I'm filled with desire,
And I just can't stop the fire.

Ooo, I get an itchin' in my heart,
Tears me all apart,
Just an itchin' in my heart—"

"All right," Lidia interrupted, lighting up a cigarette. "Let's go. Elvadine? Amber?"

"Girl, what are you trying to do?" Elvadine pronounced each syllable very slowly as if Lidia were hard of hearing.

Couldn't she see that Elvadine and Amber were finally having some fun? Lidia was always in such a hurry to get moving, even when there was no place special to go.

"I told you!" Lidia stamped her foot. "We got to get our stuff up to the lot before the boys or they're going to claim it."

"Girl, you be trippin' over nothing. So we find another lot." Elvadine shrugged. "Ooh!" she exclaimed, dipping her knee to the rhythm of the music. "This is the good part."

Lidia stared at them, too annoyed to speak. Elvadine was really getting on her nerves today, deliberately trying to make her feel bad because she didn't know the steps they had made up. Well, she wouldn't want to learn their dumb dance routine, not even if they begged her to join them, which they hadn't; though no amount of torture would get her to admit how much the noninvitation had hurt her feelings.

Finally, the song was over. Elvadine flopped to the ground and asked, "You got an extra smoke?"

"Why don't you hawk your own damn cigarettes?" Lidia said, inhaling to show how much she was enjoying her smoke.

"I risk my neck all mornin' for your dumb ass," Elvadine said resentfully. "You'd think I'm at least entitled to a five-second break and a puff of your skag."

"What do you mean, riskin' your neck?"

"What do you call trompin' around in that crazy, gap-toothed, banjo-pickin', no-eyelid, hillbilly yard, stealin' all that junk? They ever find out we robbed 'em, I reckon they gonna whup my behind 'till it be flat as yours."

"You didn't even go on their property! I'm the one who got everything," Lidia protested. It was typical of Elvadine to take credit when she didn't deserve it. She passed her the cigarette and watched her take a puff. "Quit nigger-lippin' my smoke!" she said. "Give it here!"

Elvadine yanked the cigarette out of Lidia's reach. She couldn't believe what she had just heard coming out of Lidia's mouth. "Excuse me? What the hell did you just say?"

"Gimme my smoke! What?"

"You know, I don't have to hang out with no asshole white people," she said coldly.

"What'd I do?" Lidia asked again, confused. "'Cuz I said the word nigger? That's exactly how you call all your friends."

"How I call my kind ain't none of your business. Girl, you better get out of my face."

This was no joke. Elvadine was often mad at her, but she had never sounded so serious . . . or so upset. "Okay, whatever I said, I'm sorry," Lidia apologized, eager to smooth things over between them.

Amber, who all this time had been dancing a short distance away, tuned into the tension and came rushing over. "It's a fight! What'd I miss?" she asked.

Silence. The two girls glared at each other. Lidia felt frightened. The look in Elvadine's eyes pierced through her.

"Hold on," said Elvadine. "I think you got somethin' that belongs to me. My mood ring?"

Lidia couldn't believe her ears. Elvadine had given her that ring to signify they were best friends for life. Asking for it back meant she was breaking the sacred vow of friendship they had sworn last summer, right here in these very woods.

She was not, however, about to show Elvadine how upset she was. She removed the mood ring from her finger and handed it to her. "Where's my pukka-shell necklace?" she said.

The necklace was a Christmas present from her parents, the one they had celebrated right before her father went to Vietnam. She could still remember the smile on Elvadine's face when she traded the necklace for the mood ring.

"I'll see that you get it," said Elvadine.

Lidia took the wagon handle and got ready to go. But the awful prospect of losing Elvadine's friendship—for no reason that she could understand—forced her to try again to make up. "Look," she said, scuffing her foot in the dirt. "I said I was sorry."

"What she sorry for?" Amber asked.

"Nothin'," Elvadine retorted. Tears welled up in

her eyes. She felt hurt and unrespected by the one person she had always trusted to know better. "You think that's gonna do it? You said a horrible word to me. My mamma says I don't have to hang out with nobody that denigrates me that way. Even if you are my best friend. Which you ain't, no more!"

"You can have all my cigarettes," Lidia offered, her voice small and trembling as she, too, began to cry.

Elvadine's stomach ached from the pain of Lidia's betrayal. "Oh, good. Gimme cancer to make up for it." A fly buzzed across her nose. She slapped it away with so much force that Lidia winced. "Forget it. You don't even understand what I'm sayin'."

This was a different Elvadine from the one Lidia knew and played with since she was three years old. This Elvadine sounded fierce and strong and terribly certain that she could manage perfectly well without her. Difficult as it was, Lidia realized she had no choice but to swallow her pride and ask her forgiveness.

"Maybe you're right. Maybe I don't understand, but I'll figure it out. I promise I will," she said, as the tears trickled freely down her cheeks. "'Cuz I'm gonna lose you, and you're the best friend I ever had."

"Girl, I'm the only friend you ever had. But how is a bird gonna figure out what a worm feels like? Don't even bother."

Elvadine crossed her arms against her chest

and marched off into the forest, as brave and resolute as any soldier marching off to war.

The boys spent the rest of the morning accumulating sheets of cardboard, branches, pasteboard boxes, and other miscellaneous scraps that might be useful as building materials. Their encounter with the Lipnickis was history, and they were feeling pleased with themselves as they dragged their bikes and wagon up Conner's Ridge toward the fort.

"Oh, I love to go swimmin' with big-breasted women," they sang in unison. "And swim between their legs—"

"Hey!" Marsh chortled. "Speaking of knockers, you ever wonder why Barbie has tits, but Ken doesn't have no weenie?"

"Let me ask you this, Marsh," said Chet, straight-faced. "How come you got tits and a weenie?" He poked Stu in the ribs, and they broke up laughing. They fell to the ground, slapping each other's backs, and pointing at Marsh, who tried to ignore them.

But their laughter was contagious, and soon Marsh was laughing as hard as they were. Of course, the joke was on Chet, who always wore a T-shirt to hide his fat tits. Marsh was about to point this out, when Stu crested the ridge and suddenly froze.

"Dammit!" he shouted. He threw down his bike and summoned his friends to see the horror that was unfolding just a few feet away. There were Lidia and Amber pulling a wagon of their own, quite obviously headed for the same place they were.

First the Lipnickis, now Lidia! Stu raced down the hill, cursing the day he had been born a twin.

"No way! Bull honkey, man! You said it was just gonna be us guys!" Marsh shouted, as he raced to catch up with him. "So now what are we supposed to do?"

Stu flew at his sister, ready to tackle her, punch her, do anything necessary to exclude her from his private property. Bad enough that she was always horning in on his private affairs, ruining everything he tried to do! Now, he had Marsh yelling at him, making it sound as if he had *invited* Lidia to join their gang. "This is our territory, man!" he screamed. "Get lost!"

"No way!" she yelled back at him.

Sister and brother faced off. Each of them was prepared to defend his or her right to the territory. Neither was prepared to compromise.

A moment passed, then a second. Stu sensed Chet and Marsh's impatience. They wanted to see the conflict resolved, so they could get on with their project. He knew his sister. She was more stubborn than any mule yet born. She would never back down once she had set her mind to something. He had only one chance to get rid of her.

"Race you," he challenged. "Winner gets it."

Just as he expected, Lidia nodded her agreement.

They lined up next to each other, and he counted aloud: "One, two, three."

Like two well-matched racehorses, they galloped toward the finish line—the oak tree at the far end of the field. Amber, Chet, and Marsh trailed them the entire distance. Lidia pulled ahead for a couple of seconds, but Stu quickly caught up. They ran together the rest of the way, and arrived at the tree, breathless and panting, at precisely the same second.

"Tie," Lidia gasped. "Guess we're gonna have to share it."

"This is not funny, you guys," said Marsh, coming in right behind them. "We had total dibbies on this place. Don't dibbies mean nothin' anymore?"

He may as well have sprayed gasoline on a pile of smoldering ashes. Stu and Lidia were still smarting from the beating each had taken earlier that day. They were instantly all over each other, blindly hammering and pummeling whatever body part was nearest to reach. Their friends hung back, rooting them on, but the twins heard nothing but their own angry cries.

They might have gone a full twelve rounds if Stu hadn't decided to go for a judge's ruling. Determined to win his father's sympathy, he suddenly pulled away and bolted for home. Lidia darted after him and was trailing by only a couple of seconds when he reached the house.

They found their father drinking lemonade on the front stoop. "Dad, Stu's an Indian giver!" Lidia burst out. "He said we could share the fort, and now he's goin' back on his word."

"It was my idea for the fort in the first place," Stu reminded her.

Stephen put down his glass and frowned. "Simmer down, now," he said. "Both of you screw your heads back on."

"They're drivin' us nuts!" Stu said.

"Y'all are nuts to begin with!" came Lidia's withering response.

"Not too nuts to bash your lights out!" he yelled, raising his hand to smack her.

Stephen grabbed a firm hold of his arm. "Son," he said, that one word conveying a world of meaning. Then he said, "Lidia, what time of the day they parole you from summer school this year?"

"Noon." She smirked at Stu, but her triumph was short-lived.

"All right," Stephen nodded at her. "You make sure you girls don't go to the fort beforehand and pester the daylights out of these poor boys. And Stu, when they do get there, you act like they're the most precious sight your eyes have ever seen."

Neither one was satisfied. They had each come looking to be declared the victor; instead, their father imposed a settlement. Protests of unfairness rose to their lips, but his expression made them reconsider.

"I don't want to hear about you raisin' your fists," he went on. "Y'all got that?"

"Yes, sir," they chorused.

"Whose turn to set the table? Lidia Joanne?" Lois called from the kitchen.

"I'm comin," Lidia called back to her.

Behind her father's back, she shook a warning finger at her brother. She would be at the fort tomorrow, twelve noon sharp. And Daddy would hear all about it if he didn't treat her right.

CHAPTER FOUR

FEW THINGS pleased Lidia more than to hear people say she resembled her mother. There was no doubt in her mind that after Jane Fonda, Lois Simmons was easily the most beautiful woman in America, possibly the world. Sometimes, when she was alone in the house, she would stare in the bathroom mirror, searching her reflection for points of similarity.

They both had light brown hair. But Lois' hair fell thick and straight, while Lidia's was wispy and tended to do as it pleased, even when she wore it in a ponytail. Lois had blue eyes, as clear and calm as a freshwater stream on a still summer day. Lidia's eyes were hazel-colored and generally had a worried look to them when they stared back at her from the glass.

Maybe they looked worried because she didn't like what she saw in the mirror: the gap between her teeth, the nose that seemed too big for her face. "Don't you worry," her mamma always told her when she fretted about her features. "You already have a fine brain, and you'll grow into being pretty."

No one but her mother seemed to care a hoot

about brain, and Lidia wasn't sure she could wait to be pretty. She wanted to ask her mother, had she *always* been beautiful? Or had she suddenly, one day, been magically transformed from plain to pretty?

But such a question was likely to make her mother frown with disappointment that she could be concerned with so insignificant a subject. Getting good grades at school, taking care of the house, minding her manners—that's what Lois Simmons considered important. Just because they were short on money didn't mean they had to look, sound, or behave like trash, she frequently reminded Lidia and Stu.

Lidia pulled forks and knives out of the drawer and sighed as she began to set the table. She hated to let her mother down, especially lately when she seemed so tired from working at the Dixie Queen. Things would improve as soon as her daddy got a job, which Lidia was sure he would soon do. Maybe then her parents would smile at each other and laugh the way they used to before her father had gone to Vietnam. In the meantime, though, she had to be careful about what she confided in her mother.

She sighed again, thinking of Elvadine, as she counted out four plates instead of five.

Lois was standing at the stove, her back to Lidia. But as if she could read Lidia's mind, she asked, "How come Elvadine's not comin' for supper?"

"She's not hungry," said Lidia.

"Elvadine not hungry for my sweet potatoes?" Lois chuckled. "Impossible."

"She's in a funk."

"Must be." Something in her daughter's voice told Lois there was more to the story than Lidia was admitting. She turned to look at her. "What's wrong with her, sweetie?"

Lidia carefully folded the napkins in neat triangles and placed them to the left of the plates, then said, not meeting her mother's gaze, "She asked to borrow one of my smokes—"

"You're smoking?"

"That's not what I wanted to talk about," Lidia said crossly.

Lois brandished the wooden spoon she had been using to stir the potatoes as if she wanted to turn Lidia over her knee and spank her with it. "You're gonna quit smoking right here and now or I'm gonna break all your fingers off one by one and you're gonna be smoking with stubs," she threatened. "Am I being clear enough for you?"

"Yes, ma'am," said Lidia, who knew when not to argue with her mother.

"Now, what happened to Elvadine?"

Lidia slumped down on a chair and took a deep breath. If her mamma was that mad about the smoking, what would she think, hearing about the fight? "I told her to stop nigger-lippin' my cigarette," she said, forcing the words out in a rush. Swallowing a sob, she continued, "I hurt Elvadine's feelings bad."

There were so many days when Lois felt she might burst with pride that this was her smart, beautiful, generous daughter. Yet sometimes Lidia fell so far short of her expectations. Was she asking too much of the child? Other folks in town might disagree, but Lois firmly believed that skin color or religion had no bearing on how human beings should treat one another.

She walked over to the table and put her hand under Lidia's chin. "It seems odd to me, that after almost twelve years, you don't know that the word nigger is an insult," she said.

"I do, but she calls her friends that," Lidia said miserably.

"That's her business," said Lois, sitting down next to her. She wondered whether she was responsible for Lidia's ill-chosen phrase. Perhaps she hadn't taught her well enough about prejudice— how it could destroy a person's soul and ruin lives. Perhaps teaching by example was just the beginning.

"Honey," she said gently. "That word was invented by a whole lot of ignorant people so filled with fear and hate that they had to go and make a whole other group of folks feel like they're less important in the eyes of God."

"And now I done the same?" said Lidia, her eyes filling up with tears.

"I guess you know different now, don't you?" she said, stroking Lidia's hair. She pulled her daughter close and cradled her like a baby. She needed to remember that twelve wasn't so grown up, after all.

Stephen pulled up the hood of the truck and examined its innards with a knowledgeable eye. Like a surgeon ready to commence an operation, he automatically reached for his instrument. Stu handed him the wrench and watched as Stephen unscrewed the radiator cap.

"What am I going to have to do to get you to hold yourself back?" Stephen asked, his head still stuck in the engine.

"Give me twenty dollars?" joked Stu.

"I'll give you twenty swats on the ass," Stephen said. He straightened up and glared at his son. "You think I'm kiddin'?"

"Lidia started it," said Stu, hoping to shift the blame so his father would get back to fixing the truck and talking about the war.

Stephen wondered, had he been gone so long that Stu could think he would buy such a lame excuse? It was high time he and his son got reacquainted. But first, a brief but crucial lesson. "I reckon you can give me a reason for every time you've hit your sister. Don't hit her no more." He peered at Stu's face. "She didn't split your lip, did she?"

"No, the Lipnickis did. They kicked my ass good," Stu admitted.

"Maybe they should be called the Lipkickies?" teased Stephen.

Stu grinned, enjoying the banter. "Lipdickies would be better."

"All I can tell you," Stephen said, turning more serious, "is that it only takes a split second to do something you'll regret the whole rest of your life. I can't really explain better than that." He smiled at Stu and then broke the good news he had been saving all afternoon. "I got me a job today, workin' for the state."

"Get out!" Stu exclaimed, slapping his palms together. "You serious?"

"Yes, sir," Stephen said proudly. "Your old grammar school. I'm the new custodial engineer."

"That's great! Mom!" Stu called into the house. "Dad got a janitor job at the school!"

"I heard. Isn't that wonderful?" his mother called back.

"Galdang, Dad!" Stu said, his eyes shining with happiness. "Too bad I graduated. We could hang out. That's really boss."

Stephen was touched by his son's excitement. Had he cared this much about what happened to his own father? Bryan Simmons certainly had his share of hard times, especially after the mill was closed. But they had never been especially close, and the man was dead ten years now. Stephen couldn't remember anymore if he had cheered him on during his bouts of bad luck.

He hoped he had, because it sure helped to know the kid was rooting for him. Stu seemed to understand that he needed to work not just for the money but for his self-respect.

He couldn't bear to see Lois so pale and worn. She looked more beautiful than ever to him, but he hardly felt he had the right to tell her so. He couldn't even bring himself to hug her, for fear she would break from sheer exhaustion; or worse, that she would push him away and tell him not to come near her until he could take care of his family. Not that she ever hinted at such a thing.

58

She hadn't even complained about losing their home and having to live in this miserable excuse for a house. But she acted so quiet and still ever since his return that he didn't know what she was thinking and was afraid to ask.

Well, that situation was about to change or his name was not Stephen Simmons. He had a job now—steady work with decent pay. Soon, they would be all caught up on their debts and saving money every week for a decent place to live. It was a promise he made to himself the day he came back from the hospital and stood with Stu, staring at the devastation that once had been their home.

"We're gonna get us a real house and everything will be just fine again." He made the same promise now to his son. "You wait and see."

They celebrated his new job with a special treat of ice-cream sodas for dessert. Then Stu helped Lois with the dishes while Stephen sat outside with Lidia watching the summer sky slowly darken and the stars appear. After awhile, Lois and Stu joined them on the stoop, and the children plied him with questions about the war.

Lois sat in silence. Their bodies didn't touch, but he could feel her next to him, inches away, her arms folded around her bent legs, her head resting on her knees. She let the kids do all the talking, but he could feel her listening intently to every word. She hardly moved, except when Stu asked how it felt to kill someone; then she reached over and lightly tapped his arm, as if to warn him against saying too much.

When they began to yawn and bicker with each other, Lois sent them off to bed. She herself went inside a few minutes later, complaining of the mosquitoes. Stephen sat alone, unbothered by the tiny buzzing creatures after the ferocious, blood-sucking insects he had encountered in the combat zone. He watched the moon rise, welcoming the momentary quiet, reflecting on the fact that the one question his kids hadn't asked was whether he had ever been scared.

When Jimmy Owen came lurching up the road, screaming drunk, Stephen decided it was time to follow his wife into the house. He found her sitting in the kitchen, the newspaper on her lap, tiredly staring into space. He bent to kiss her cheek, and she looked up, startled, then smiled wanly, as if even her face muscles were too tired to respond properly. Stephen decided against the kiss and went to check on the children.

Stu lay on his side, hugging his pillow, one arm outstretched. He was fast asleep, and his face looked peaceful as a baby's. Stephen pulled up the sheet he had kicked off and kissed him. When he turned to Lidia's bed, he saw that she was still awake.

"Dad?" she whispered, propping her head on her hand. "How come you and Mom don't talk no more like you used to?"

He was stunned by her perception. Was the distance between Lois and himself so obvious? He sat down on the side of her bed and whispered, "I've been gone a long time, Lidia. We're just givin' each other a little space right now."

Her eyes gleamed in the moonlight that slanted through the open window. Suddenly, he could see in her face the beautiful, loving woman she would grow up to be.

"You better start crowdin' her, Dad. You gotta put your arms around the woman once in a while or she's gonna think you don't like her no more," she said in a low voice, so as not to wake up Stu. "Now, I have to give you this advice, 'cuz I can see you just don't know what you're doin'."

"I'm gonna have to take that to heart," he said earnestly, wondering how the heck his daughter had gotten to be so wise at such a young age.

"Good. If you need me, I'm here." She yawned as her head hit the pillow. "I'm glad you're bein' the janitor. You're gonna make that old school sparkle. Good night, Daddy," she mumbled and was instantly asleep.

He kissed her cheek and left the room, gently shutting the door behind him. Lois looked up as he tiptoed into the kitchen. The moonlight glowed at his back, framing him in a golden radiance that brought a smile to her lips. There had been so many days when she felt as if she couldn't breathe for missing him. Raising the kids on her own was hard, but she got used to being both mother and father. The tough part was living through each day and night without hearing Stephen's voice, seeing his smile, feeling his hands on her skin. And the worst was not knowing; watching the terrible news of the war every night on TV—with its grisly images of battle and brain-numbing casualty numbers—and praying that he was still alive.

She couldn't imagine loving any other man. She had thanked the Lord from her heart to have him back in one piece, and now that the nightmares were gone, she had even more to be grateful for. Though she wasn't superstitious, she believed in the power of fate; and fate had meant for her and Stephen to be together, which was why his coldness towards her felt so painful.

In her worst moments, she worried that he had fallen out of love but was afraid to tell her because he knew it would break her heart. But something in her counseled patience. She couldn't begin to imagine what he had been through, the massacres he might have witnessed. Her father said that war forced a man to walk down roads that forever changed his soul. It could take a long time, her father said, for a man to find his way back home.

Stephen switched on the radio and fumbled with the dial. He stopped when he found the kind of music he had been searching for; the sweetly seductive voice of Percy Sledge, singing "When a Man Loves a Woman." Turning the volume down low, he extended his hand to Lois with a mock flourish and said, "Lidia suggested that I dance with you. That is, if you're still interested in takin' my hands?"

Her eyes glistened with unshed tears as she stood up and rested her head on his shoulder. "I've been waitin' on you to ask for the longest time," she said.

They swayed in each other's arms, oblivious to everything but the joy of the moment, of rediscovering their secret, unspoken language. They didn't hear the children's bedroom door creak open. Nor did they notice Lidia peeking through the crack, smiling with the satisfaction gained from the knowledge of a job well done.

Awakened by the music, Stu opened his eyes and saw his sister spying on his parents. "Leave them alone, now, will you?" he whispered.

Lidia shook her head. "I wasn't doin' nothin, just makin' sure they're dancin' properly." But for once, she took his advice. She quietly closed the door and climbed back into bed.

She slowly drifted off to sleep, thinking that she couldn't remember when she had ever seen her mamma cry from happiness. Or maybe—though she hoped this wasn't so—her mamma was crying because her daddy kept stepping on her toes. What mattered was that her daddy had taken her advice. Things were finally getting back to the way they were supposed to be. Now all she had to worry about was making up with Elvadine.

CHAPTER FIVE

"GOOD MORNING, girls and boys."

The bell had just rung on the first day of summer school. Lidia's new teacher stood at the front of the room, aiming her pointer at the words she had written in careful script on the blackboard.

She cleared her throat to signal them to silence, then announced, "My name is Miss Strapford. Notice the anterior letters? 'S' is for steel." She punctuated her statement by stabbing the chalk into a period and underlined the next four letters, "T-R-A-P. In the event that any of you consider cheating in this class, that's where you'll land . . . in my trap."

The classroom was hot and overcrowded, and many of the children, including Lidia, sat fanning themselves with folded pieces of notebook paper. But it was Miss Strapford, not the heat, that was preoccupying them. Teachers were supposed to be middle-aged, plump, and dumpy.

Miss Strapford, however, had a mass of brassy blond hair piled on top of her head. She was wearing heels so high they could have passed for stilts, and a tight sleeveless dress whose buttons strained across her very generous chest. Except in the movies, they had never seen any one who looked quite like her.

Elvadine, who was sitting right behind Lidia, leaned over to Amber and grinned. "That woman got the biggest tee-taws I ever seen," she whispered. "I suspect a man could fall out a ten-story window, land on them things, and bounce clean to the moon. Her brassiere ever burst, she could wipe out the whole front row by giving them all whiplash."

"Excuse me!" Miss Strapford rapped on her desk with the pointer. "Darling, when a teacher is speaking, the polite thing for girls and boys to do is to shut their little mouths and listen. Understand?"

"Yes, ma'am." Elvadine nodded, barely suppressing a giggle.

Miss Strapford perched herself on the edge of her desk and swung her high heels, causing Lester Lucket, seated near the front, to swallow his chewing gum. She primly folded her hands and said, "This summer we are going to be familiarizing ourselves with what I believe is just the finest little book ever come into print. It is entitled *Why My Life Is Like a Bowl of Cherries.* Doesn't that title just give you a thrill?"

As if to answer her own question, a strange panting sound—something between a wheeze and a groan—suddenly erupted from her throat. Her students, more embarrassed than thrilled by her display of emotion, secretly exchanged worried glances. Lidia half-turned to wink at Elvadine.

But Elvadine looked away, rejecting her attempt to make peace.

"Once we finish this book," Miss Strapford continued, "we are going to be devoting our time to writing our memoirs. This is where you will indicate to me why your life is like a bowl of cherries. Everybody has dog turds in their back yard. The proper thing is to cultivate the roses so you can't smell the crap. The first thing is, let's try to get this class in some sort of order."

She pointed to a black student sitting in the front row. "Son, you're a tall boy. Why don't you swap seats with that little girl back there in the red? Go on, pick up your stuff and move on back."

Scrutinizing the room, she picked out another black student, who had also chosen a desk to the front. "And you with the hearing aid," she said. "Why don't you take a seat back there? If you can't hear, you just crank that little thing up."

Next, Miss Strapford's gaze settled on Elvadine. She clapped her hands and said, "Oh, my, you're a big girl! I'm sure you'll see just fine in the rear aisle. Go on. Now you, little girl." She pointed to Lidia. "Why don't you have a seat up front?"

Lidia and Elvadine reluctantly gathered up their belongings and obeyed their teacher's instructions. Miss Strapford spent the next several minutes rearranging her students, until she had the room perfectly segregated with all the black children seated in the back.

"Isn't this much better?" she trilled. "I can see all your faces so much more clearly."

Lidia turned and scanned the faces of the black

students. Elvadine was staring out the window, her eyes focused on some far distant point. Amber looked bored, as if she were too used to this sort of treatment from white folks to pay it much heed. "Now to go on with what I was saying. . . ." She opened her book and flipped through it, apparently searching for a particular page.

Lester, whose desk was now right next to Lidia's, bent over and whispered to her, "Nigger-lover."

"Shut up!" she hissed.

"Colored girl!" Miss Strapford barked at Elvadine. "Didn't I just tell you to hush up?"

It took a few moments for Elvadine to realize that Miss Strapford was speaking to her. "I wasn't saying nothin'," she flatly informed the teacher.

"Well, I distinctly heard you whispering. Go stand in the hallway until I say you can join the class again."

Elvadine stood up slowly. She had such a hopeless look on her face that Lidia felt compelled to defend her. "But ma'am." She raised her hand. "She's tryin' to tell you she didn't—"

"Hush!" Miss Strapford glared at her. "I am not speaking to you!" She shifted her gaze back to Elvadine. "Tell the class what was so important that you had to interrupt me again."

"I told you, I didn't say nothin'," Elvadine said in a low voice, sounding as ashamed of herself as if she were indeed guilty.

Miss Strapford tapped her pointer across her knees. "I know you did say something," she insisted. "And I want to hear what it was. We're all waiting."

"She already told you," Lidia said, her temper rising the more Miss Strapford continued to pick on Elvadine.

"She can speak for herself," Miss Strapford snapped.

By now, every pair of eyes was fixed on Elvadine. Lidia watched her gnawing on her thumbnail, obviously mortified by all the attention. She could tell that Elvadine was also getting angrier by the minute. Any second, her temper would reach its boiling point. She would open her mouth and let loose with whatever she was thinking.

Sure enough, Elvadine nodded her head, as if she had made up her mind about something important. Miss Strapford had already shamed her so badly in front of her classmates that it didn't matter what she said. With so much shame exposed, she had nothing to lose. She could even go ahead and tell the truth.

"All right," she said loudly. "I'll tell you. I was sayin', Elvadine, what you got to write about? I been in the sixth grade my whole good-for-nothin' life. Ain't got no daddy. Don't go nowhere but where my feet takes me. Only money ever belong to me in the whole world was twenty dollars I got myself in a birthday card from my uncle last year. But it wasn't really for my birthday. Really it was for layin' over his lap and lettin' him spank me with my underpants down."

Lidia gasped. She had helped Elvadine spend every penny of that twenty dollars on movies, comic books, candy, and clothes for their doll babies. But Elvadine never told her the true reason for her uncle's generosity. The other children were staring open-mouthed at Elvadine. A few looked like they were barely containing their laughter, but most seemed so shocked by her honesty that they could hardly move.

Elvadine took a deep breath and went on, her voice strong and steady. "Now, here you come along, shoving me in the back of the room where I can't even see good, which means I'm probably not gonna graduate this summer neither. And just 'cuz you read how some white man says life is like a bowl of cherries, I got to come up with somethin' gonna fit his sayin'. Well, that's fine. I'll just write down how happy I'm gonna be to get twenty more dollars on my birthday, never mind what he got planned for me this year. And I'm gonna write how maybe the new man my mamma is seein' might stop drinkin' and treat me nice. And maybe he gonna adopt me and take us off the welfare. And at the end, I'm gonna be sure to put, 'Life sure is a bowl full o' cherries.' But to tell you the truth, Miss Strapford, I think you and that book and this whole class be a bowl full of mess."

The room was absolutely still. Even Miss Strapford seemed momentarily at a loss for words. But she quickly recovered herself and said, "Pick yourself up and go out in the hallway."

"Didn't you hear a damn thing she said?" cried Lidia.

"Excuse me?"

Lidia was past caring whether Elvadine stopped being her friend or how Miss Strapford might punish her for speaking up. She knew she had to teach her teacher the lesson she so recently learned from her mother.

"She told you the best truth she knows," she said, forcing herself not to cry. "And you don't got any right to put her out, or call her a liar, neither. My ma says, folks who treat strangers bad only do it because they are ignorant, so I'm gonna help you. Elvadine's gonna sit up here beside me from now on, where she can see. And she's not gonna go by 'colored girl' no more. You're gonna learn her name. I don't know about you, but all of my friends have names. And it just so happens this is my best friend. Her name is Elvadine."

Miss Strapford's cheeks had turned bright red, and her eyes seemed about to bulge out of their sockets. She grabbed Lidia by the back of her neck, marched her and Elvadine out of the room, and ordered them to report to the principal. She would be along shortly to give a full accounting of their crimes, she said. In the meantime, they were not to move a muscle. And they were to keep their mouths shut. As far as she was concerned, they had already said enough to get them permanently expelled.

Lidia and Elvadine sat next to each other on the wooden bench outside the principal's office. Lidia felt both scared and exhilarated, the same way she felt riding the roller coaster at the county fair. She had broken a cardinal rule: Thou shalt not speak disrespectfully to a teacher. But Miss Strapford didn't deserve her respect. She hoped the principal would understand. She had no doubt her mamma would.

She and Elvadine still hadn't said a word to each other, and she wondered what Elvadine was thinking. She wanted in the worst way to reach over and give Elvadine a hug. She deserved a medal, really, for being so brave. But Miss Strapford had said not to move, and Lidia didn't dare make the situation worse than it already was.

Suddenly, though, she felt Elvadine's hand on hers. She saw that Elvadine had taken off her mood ring and silently placed it in Lidia's palm. Lidia quickly slipped it onto her finger and felt her face break into an ear-to-ear smile. Without even looking, she knew that Elvadine was wearing the very same smile. Who cared if they got expelled? Elvadine had forgiven her. They were best friends again.

The fort was beginning to take shape. The first step had been to lay a wooden plank foundation across the V formed by two sturdy branches in the trunk of the ancient oak tree. Next, they were building upwards from the base, throwing up walls and a second story that would be the lookout tower.

The three girls had arrived exactly at noon to claim their right to participate. Amber had brought her daddy's hammer, and now she was busy pounding nails into the boards, singing as she worked.

"I been workin' on the railroad, all the live-long day—"

"Excuse me, fat girl," Marsh interrupted her. "Is it absolutely necessary that you serenade us?"

Amber frowned. "I'm on a diet, I hope you

know!" she retorted. "'Cuz I got a granular condition."

"You got a Hostess Twinkie's condition, is what you got," Marsh said. Then he lowered his voice and told Stu, "These girls are killin' me, man. Let's eighty-six 'em!"

Stu looked up from the nails he had been sorting. "I promised my dad we wouldn't."

"Ooh, well, gee, wowee," Marsh razzed him. "Wouldn't wanna break a promise to your old man."

Chet nodded at the board that Marsh had been working on. "Least they can drive nails in straight," he said. "Who taught you to hammer like that? Helen Keller?"

"Hey, can I help it if they were warped?"

"My nails are okay," Amber said smugly.

"Who asked you, blubber-butt?" Marsh threw down his hammer, appraising the piles of material they had collected. He said, "We need some more junk if we're gonna build a real fort."

Stu sat back on his heels, recalling his father's warning to treat Lidia nicely. He couldn't stop Marsh from picking on the girls, but maybe he could get them out of the way, at least temporarily. Besides, Marsh was right, they did need more junk.

The plan came to him immediately; it was brilliant. "This will never work, Lidia," he said. "We need a boss. What do you say, we go double or nothin' on a dare. Winner gets to run the show here, loser has to follow orders?"

"Stu?" Chet said, as if to say, are you nuts?

Stu ignored him and waited to see if Lidia would take the bait.

She hesitated a second, then said, "Fine. What's the dare?"

"We'll make a list of junk. If you can't get it, we're the boss and you have to do exactly what we say."

Lidia nodded confidently. After what she and Elvadine had been through, there was nothing they couldn't accomplish, especially with Amber on their team. Contrary to Miss Strapford's prediction, they hadn't been expelled, only suspended for a week. The principal warned that next time, "though there better not be a next time," he said, they would be out for good. But Lidia had gotten the impression that he was not pleased with Miss Strapford's behavior, either. Maybe he also threatened to kick Miss Strapford out of the school if she behaved so meanly to her students again.

Stu conferred with his pals. "Okay. What do we need?"

"Nudie cards?" Marsh suggested.

"It's got to be for the fort, Marsh," said Stu, starting a list of things the girls would never find.

"A machine gun," said Marsh. "A real one with ammo."

Stu sighed and kept on writing. Finally, he handed it to Lidia, who looked it over with Elvadine. She shook her head. "A doughboy pool? No way."

"All right," Stu said. "But everything else."

"How we gonna get a stove?" asked Elvadine.

Stu shrugged. "That's your problem. And girls? We need it today."

An hour later, when they decided to take a break from their work, the boys were still laughing and congratulating Stu on his scheme. Equipped with a raft-shaped sheet of cardboard, they hiked over to the top of the nearest ridge.

"Think they'll get any of it?" Marsh asked.

"Hell, no. They're probably at Elvadine's having a back-bend contest or something stupid like that," scoffed Stu, positioning himself on the cardboard sheet behind Chet and Marsh.

They pushed hard with their hands to get themselves going, then went screaming and skidding wildly down the steep, grassy hill. They flew the last few inches to the bottom, then brushed themselves off and started back up the hill for another ride.

Chet pointed to a second hill they had never tried before. "Let's slide down over there. It's steeper."

"No way," said Stu. "There's a big hole there and that wood that's covering it is so rotten it'll break through."

"You're jivin' me!" Chet said, pleased for once to be playing the daredevil.

Marsh strained to move the huge piece of plywood that lay at the base of the hill. With some effort, he maneuvered it off to the side and lifted it up. A horrible stench instantly filled the air.

"That stinks, man!" Chet yelled, holding his nose.

"Livin' breathin' Jesus!" Marsh exclaimed. "One time through here, we'd die of fumigation. Must be a cesspool. Stu's right."

Chet grinned, grabbed the cardboard sled, and ran full speed up the hill.

"Hey! It's my turn to go alone!" Stu shouted, taking off after him.

Chet reached the top before Stu had a chance to catch up. But instead of starting back down again, he signaled his friends to stay put. "Lipnickis are comin'," he called down to them.

Stu stared at Chet. Then he stared at the plywood. "Are you thinkin' what I think you're thinkin?" Chet asked him.

Stu nodded. "Yep. They can't see it from up there. C'mon!"

The three boys raced back to the hole. "This'll make them feel at home," said Stu, pulling the plywood off the pit and shoving it as far to the side as he could manage; then, they ran back up the first hill, screaming with laughter as they contemplated their revenge.

They sailed down again, still laughing. When they turned to walk back up, they found four of the Lipnickis watching them from the top of the ridge. "This is our territory now!" Arliss shouted. "Get lost! And leave the cardboard!"

"What isn't your territory?" Stu yelled.

"Only what we don't want and this here hill we want."

Stu spread out his arms. "Take it. It's all yours. If I were you, though, I wouldn't go down that hill. It's too steep."

"Well, you ain't us, are you?" Leo taunted them. "We can go down any old hill we please!"

"Suit yourselves. But don't say I didn't tell you so," said Stu, winking at his pals.

"Yeah, you're not the boss of us. We're the boss of you!" Ula screamed while Leo hustled down the hill and grabbed the cardboard away from Chet. The boys watched as he rejoined his family and then walked over to the section of the hill that Stu had warned them about. Laughing and shouting, they all crowded onto the cardboard, shoved off, and soared straight towards the open pit.

Now it was the boys' turn to crow as the Lipnickis vanished from sight. They heard screams, a loud thud, then coughing and retching.

"This is disgusting stinkin' crap!" yelled Leo from somewhere far below them.

"That does it, Simmons!" Arliss' voice came floating up to them. "I'm gonna kick your ass for this! This is war!"

"Take a bath first. That way we won't be able to smell you comin', turd brains," Stu yelled.

He didn't bother waiting around to hear their response.

With Elvadine objecting every step of the way, Lidia headed right for the Lipnickis' place. If Stu and his friends figured she was going to let them boss her around, they could darn well figure again. They thought they were so smart, but their dumb old list didn't scare her a bit; nor did Mr. Lipnicki or any of his dirty-faced kids. She would outsmart them all, and then she and Elvadine and Amber would be giving the orders around the fort.

She grinned in anticipation as they knelt behind a patch of bushes that gave a clear view of the Lipnickis' yard.

"I told you," Elvadine whined. "I ain't never comin' back here."

"Elvadine, this is the only place in the whole town with this much unrotted junk," Lidia reminded her.

"What if that white man, Lipnicki, comes out and shoots us?"

Lidia shook her head impatiently. "He ain't gonna shoot us. Why would you even think something like that?"

"'Cuz if I was him, I'd shoot us. And if I was white, I'd probably aim for me," Elvadine said flatly.

Lidia could see there was some logic to her argument, but she wasn't about to admit that to Elvadine. Their only hope for control of the fort lay a few tempting feet away, on the other side of the fence.

"Ain't nobody even home. Trust me," she said. To prove she was right, she boldly stood up and walked over to the fence. No one called out to her to stop. Nothing moved except the chipmunks scurrying about collecting nuts. Wherever the Lipnickis were, it certainly wasn't here.

She quickly scaled the fence, dropped into the yard, and took a good look around. The very first things she saw lying on the ground were a large roll of corrugated tin and a stove that took her but a moment to recognize.

"This is all our stuff from the old house," she indignantly informed Elvadine and Amber, who had come scrambling after her. She bent down and picked up a brick. "It's our damn fireplace."

"How'd it get all the way here?" Amber asked.

"Shoot. I bet that crazy hillbilly man stole everything left in your old house after that man with the bulldozer knocked it down," said Elvadine. She glanced around nervously, waiting for her fears to materialize in the form of Mr. Lipnicki or one of his sons carrying a rifle cocked and ready to shoot.

"Wait 'til the guys hear," said Amber.

Lidia smiled victoriously. "With this stuff, we rule the roost. C'mon, let's get what we got to and go."

Suddenly she heard sounds coming from somewhere between where they were standing and the Lipnickis' house. She put her finger to her mouth to caution her friends to be quiet, then motioned them to follow her. Elvadine rolled her eyes . . . she had *warned* Lidia, but the girl would never listen. As they hurriedly hid behind a tall pile of discarded tires, Lidia grabbed a piece of pipe for protection.

The noise got louder. It was coming directly toward them. Lidia couldn't make out who or what she was hearing, and she didn't want to be discovered cowering behind the tires. Holding the pipe above her head so she was ready to strike, she jumped out and confronted her foe.

It was none other than little Billy Lipnicki, who was all of five years old. As usual, he looked like he had been dipped in a tub of dirt; his clothes were stained with filth, cereal flakes clung to his hair, gobs of dirt were crusted around his mouth, and his nose was running like a water fountain.

He took one look at Lidia, screamed in terror, and ran like a scared bobcat. But Lidia was too fast for him. She caught him in a second and grabbed hold of his shirt.

"Don't be scared," she tried to reassure him as he squirmed in her grip. "I'm not gonna harm you. My name's Lidia, and this here's Amber and Elvadine. Don't you wanna make friends? I'll let you go if you promise not to scream anymore."

She dropped her hands and examined him more closely. She felt sorry for the little boy, especially when he turned his head and cringed, almost as if he expected her to hit him.

"I know you think we're stealin' your daddy's property, but this here junk used to be part of my old house," she explained. "The city plowed my house down, and your daddy must have hauled it all off here. You understand that? I'm gonna take what's rightfully mine, but you gotta promise not to say a word to your brothers and sisters. You promise?"

Billy stared silently at her.

"Maybe his daddy sawed off his tongue," said Elvadine.

"Elvadine! Don't say those things! Can't you see he's impressionable?" Lidia chided. Then she asked, "Either of you bring any money?"

Amber shook her head.

"I only got ten cents," Elvadine said.

Ten cents was enough. Lidia held out her hand.

"Oh, no. I got to save this for my mamma's birthday. I promised to buy her a Butterfinger."

"I seen your mamma and she doesn't need another Butterfinger."

"She needs a Butterfinger more than you need my ten cents," said Elvadine stubbornly.

Lidia kept her hand outstretched and tapped her foot, waiting for Elvadine to give in. She would eventually; she could never say no to Lidia. Sure enough, after a minute or two of crossing her arms across her chest and shaking her head, Elvadine fished the dime out of her pocket and made a big production of handing it over to Lidia.

Lidia held up the coin like a medal and waved it in front of Billy's nose. "Tell you what," she said. "You promise to keep quiet about us comin' here, and we'll give you ten cents, every trip."

"Hey, you guys!" Marsh announced. "Dig this!"

The boys had taken a shortcut through the woods. They had almost reached the turnoff to the fort when Marsh spotted an oversized hornet's nest dangling from a tree on the side of the road. Chet and Stu caught up with him and stopped to observe the insects buzzing around their cone-shaped nest.

"What if," said Marsh, "a bunch of blind kids were havin' a birthday party and they thought it was a piñata?" He slapped his thigh and chuckled at the image. "They'd be bashin' it with a stick, and instead of candy, billions of hornets would come flyin' out and ruin the whole party! Oh, man! What a gut-buster!"

Sometimes Marsh could be as big a jerk as the Lipnickis. "You think hornets attacking blind kids is funny?" Stu asked incredulously.

"Yeah," said Marsh, cracking up.

"It doesn't even make sense," said Chet. "What kind of parents would let their kids play with a hornet's nest?"

"Maybe they can't afford a real piñata. You ever think of that?"

"No," said Chet, still trying to puzzle out Marsh's idea.

Stu had walked on ahead and reached the end of the road, beyond which lay the fort. "Oh, no!" he groaned, hardly believing what his eyes were seeing.

The girls had spread out their loot at the foot of the oak tree. Somehow, they had managed to find every last item on his list.

"Start building. We're the bosses now." Lidia gloated as the boys traipsed up the path.

"We'll build it with their stuff, and then we'll kick them out," Marsh whispered to Stu.

"Can't. We promised," Stu said gloomily.

"We'll have to build it with iron to support Amber," Chet jeered.

"After you build it, then paint it real good," Lidia said, savoring her victory over Stu. She pretended to consider the outside of the fort, then said, "Yeah. Why don't one of you boys go see if you can find some nice pink paint?"

Stu could have killed her. She was making a fool of him *and* landing him in trouble with his friends. It was like he always said: Every time he looked around, there she was following him.

Whcn he grew up, he was going to move far enough away so that he would never have to see her again. But for now, he had just one thing to say to her: "Don't push your luck, muffin mouth."

CHAPTER SIX

STEPHEN FELT about as old and tired as his battered wreck of a car, which had threatened to stall on him the whole way home from work. He pulled into his driveway and turned the key. The engine screeched in protest before it rumbled ominously and died. Stephen sighed; this would be a hell of a time for Flossy to quit on him.

He climbed out of the car and noticed Jimmy Owen stretched out on his stoop, his cigarette glowing in the dark like a beacon summoning home the weary traveler. Stephen waved, and Jimmy saluted him with his bottle. He had almost made it safely into the house when, as if on cue, Mrs. Higgens appeared in her doorway.

"Think you can make any more noise with that damn car of yours?" she demanded.

"Sorry about that, Mrs. Higgens," he said, stepping into the house.

"And quit tryin' to look through my dress to see my nipples!" she yelled after him.

He thought, *In your dreams, Mrs. Higgens,* and chuckled to himself. He owed her one, he supposed, for giving him a laugh when all he wanted to do was cry. At least the old witch still had her fantasies, which was more than could be said for himself and too many other folks he knew.

The house was quiet, the kids already asleep. He went into the bedroom, sank down onto the bed, and pulled off his boots. Lost in thought, he didn't realize Lois had come in until she kissed the back of his neck and asked, "How was your day, hon?"

He had spent the last hour trying to figure out how best to tell her. Finally he decided there was no way to soften the news. "They let me go from the job today," he said, as she slipped under the covers.

Shocked, she stopped in mid-motion. "Why? It hasn't even been a week."

His head ached from dreading this moment all afternoon and evening. He felt angry, too. It was getting so he couldn't tell the difference between how he saw himself and how the people in charge saw him. The evidence of his failure—as a friend, father, husband, provider—was all around him.

"Some way or another they found out I spent time in that mental hospital," he said.

"You tell them you went into that hospital voluntarily? For nightmares?" she asked, moving over to hold him.

He repeated what his supervisor had told him earlier in the day. "It's nothin' personal, they said. Law says you can't work for the city or state within the vicinity of children if you spent time in a mental facility or a corrective institution."

"It's on account of our government you wound up in that place, and now the state's turnin' you down for work, like you're some kind of criminal!" she exploded.

He felt her arms tighten around him. Then she said, more calmly, "This is crazy! We still got my job, and we can get food stamps."

"God bless America," he said bitterly. "They give you a handout before they give you a job. No food stamps, please."

"You'll find a job," she assured him.

He prayed she was right. "I will. But don't tell the children just yet. I just don't want them gettin' the idea the world's against us," he said.

He fell quiet, recalling how happy they had both been about his custodial job. He had to set them a better example than the one he'd had as a boy. Even now, it was painful to remember.

"My father, he used to say, nothin' you ever do in your lifetime is gonna make a difference. Don't you know, Lois, out of all the remarks anybody ever said to me, that's the one I held onto. Maybe that's why I joined up when they were drafting . . . my chance to do something good. And then I let my best friend die because I didn't have enough guts and self-respect to stand up and. . . ."

His voice faltered as he lost himself in his memories.

"Don't do yourself like this," Lois said softly. "You did the only thing you knew."

Had he? How could she know that? How could anyone who hadn't been there even know how it felt? He had been over this ground before, with her as well as with the doctors at the hospital. The doctors had told him he needed to forgive himself. People died in battle. He wasn't responsible for what had happened. Stephen listened and pretended to agree, but he knew differently. He could have changed things if only he had tried harder. A person had to make the effort. If you let go of hope, you might as well be dead.

"I don't want our children growing up thinking they're powerless because of me," he said, wiping the tears from his face. "Everything they do in this world has a consequence. Our children still believe in miracles; they still believe anything is possible. And so long as they believe that way, they're gonna be something. They're gonna make a difference in this world—and that means I made a difference."

Lois fell asleep holding him. Stephen heard her deep, even breathing as he lay wide awake, flipping through the mental images that haunted his days and nights. He thought that once he was home and working, busy with Lois and the kids, his memories of the war would fade. But they kept popping back into his head, reminding him of the self he had left behind in Vietnam.

Tonight, sleep seemed impossible. After awhile, he gave up trying and went to read on the living-room couch. Lidia's school notebook had fallen on the floor. He picked it up and read the heading at the top of the first page: "Why My Life Is Like a Bowl of Cherries."

The rest of the page was blank. He was sorry. He wished he could have read her answer. He couldn't imagine how she would have come up with such a notion, but he hoped she truly meant it.

He fished out *Time* magazine from between two cushions and read an article about hippies. He studied the pictures of the hippies dressed in crazy colored rags, then noticed to his horror that Stu and Lidia were there among the crowds of kids who had hitched across America to San Francisco. Dodge was there, too, gesturing him to join them. "It's better than 'Nam, man," Dodge shouted, as Stephen suddenly realized he had lost his rifle.

Then Lidia waved to him from across a corn field that was littered with corpses. "You ain't havin' no nightmares, are you?" she said.

Lidia's hand was on his shoulder when he woke up. Disoriented, he looked around and remembered he was still in Ambertree. "Yeah, I guess I was," he said, relieved to see she was wearing her shorty pajamas, rather than the hippie clothes from his dream. "I'm sorry to wake you."

She sat down next to him on the couch and said anxiously, "You're not going away again, are you? Stu says you had a trauma syndrome of some sort."

He hid a smile, thinking that his kids were too damn smart for their own good. "I'm not going anywhere tonight, but you're going back to sleep, firecracker," he said, tweaking her ponytail.

"Pick me up," she said agreeably.

She was heavier than he expected. He kept forgetting that she was no longer his little baby girl who toddled after him wherever he went from the first minute she learned to walk. She nestled her head against his chest and found his lucky pen in his shirt pocket. "How long since you had this angel pen?" she asked, shaking it so that the angel suspended inside the vial of liquid was floating up and down.

"Since I was a boy," he said, telling her what she already knew.

"Do I have a guardian angel?" she asked sleepily.

He kissed the top of her head and smelled the sunshine in her hair. "Lidia, I bet you have a dozen of them."

"I wish you were mine," she murmured. "You understand me better than anyone else in the whole world."

"Well, someday, when I'm old and gray and the Lord calls me home, maybe I'll just ask him about that job," he said.

"And you'll look out for Stu, too?"

"Yes, and Stu, too," he whispered.

Comforted and ready for sleep, Lidia gave him back the pen.

"Keep it," he said, pressing it into her hand. She was fast asleep by the time her head hit the pillow.

Stephen tiptoed out to rejoin Lois in bed. This time, he, too, feel asleep immediately.

Stephen invited Stu to come for a ride, just the two of them. He had a surprise, he said. And no, he wasn't giving any hints about what it was. Stu could try and guess if he wanted to, or he could wait until they got there. Stephen wasn't about to spill the beans. A surprise meant no telling.

They had driven only a few miles when Stephen turned down a dirt road that ran parallel to the tracks. He stopped the car and pointed to the nearest house. No amount of guessing could have prepared Stu for his father's announcement. Someday soon, he told Stu, that house was going to be theirs.

"I have to warn you, though," he said, as Stu bolted out of the car. "Her roof's brand new. Checked beneath her, she's copper-piped through and through, and I'll be damned if I can find a single leak. Poor thing ain't got an ounce of character. I don't know if we could live with that."

Stu gaped at the two-story, white-frame house, which was shaded by tall elm trees and surrounded on three sides by open fields. It was smaller than the old house, but newer and much more solid looking. "How're we gonna afford her?" he asked skeptically.

Stephen grinned. "She's been repossessed. Found out today, the bank's had her on the market fourteen months. Nobody's interested in her, on account of she's so close to the train tracks. Tragic, isn't it?"

"You got money hidden away you ain't been tellin' us about?"

"No."

Stu felt a sudden, sickening fear in his belly that his father was having hallucinations on account of his trauma syndrome. "I don't understand," he said suspiciously. "How will you be able to buy her, working as a janitor?"

"Well, I won't," Stephen said. "I'm gonna get another job, a better one, and that's how I'll pay for her."

The pain in Stu's belly worsened. "Did you lose the janitor job?"

"Yes, I did," Stephen said. He always believed in telling his kids the truth, even if it was unpleasant, and the boy would find out eventually. He quickly added, "That's just a temporary setback. But I won't give up, not ever. Neither should you. Come around back."

An enormous oak tree, its gnarled branches stretching to an upper-story window, stood guard over the back of the house. "Up there's gonna be your room. Care to take a gander?" Stephen asked.

Stu felt torn between worrying that his daddy wasn't altogether in his right mind and wanting more than anything in the world to believe him. He studied his father's face. He wasn't foaming at the mouth or rolling his eyes, both of which Stu figured to be signs of lunacy. He had never before promised anything that he didn't deliver. Obviously, he knew what he was talking about when he said the house would be theirs.

That settled, Stu joyfully scampered after Stephen up the tree and out onto one of the branches. They peered through the window at the room that Stephen had designated as Stu's.

"You even get your own desk built in over there," Stephen said, pointing to the far corner.

"And you can climb out this window and down the tree any time you like."

Stu crawled over the ledge and pressed his eyes against the window pane. Then he noticed that the window was unlocked. He looked hopefully at his father.

Stephen shrugged. "Ah, hell. I reckon nobody'll care if we tromp around in her, long as we don't dirty anything."

They forced open the window and climbed inside the spacious, sun-drenched room. "Dang! It's the biggest room I ever seen," Stu said, luxuriating in the idea of having it all to himself, without Lidia monitoring his every move.

Together, they explored the rest of the upstairs rooms. When they reached the stairs, Stephen surprised himself and Stu by hopping onto the polished wooden bannister and sliding down to the ground floor. Stu whooped with delight and hurtled after him.

The kitchen was to the left of the staircase. It was bigger and sunnier than their old kitchen and filled with gleaming white appliances.

Stephen laughed as Stu opened the refrigerator door and inspected the cabinets. "Take a good look," he said. "Once your mom and your sister move in here with that fryin' skillet, it's never gonna be the same."

On the other side of the house, past the living room, was the master bedroom, which had the same view as Stu's room just above. Stephen's eyes lit up and a smile spread across his face when he spotted the dressing area next to the window.

"She always wanted her very own vanity," he said, smoothing his hand over the delicate little table.

Stu didn't hear him. His attention had been caught by something much more interesting than his mother's vanity—the tire swing that hung from one of the trees. It swayed lazily in the late afternoon breeze, summoning him for a ride. He hurried outside, hopped on the swing, and pumped his legs to work up some momentum. Then he noticed an odd marking on the tree trunk. Moving closer to get a better look, he read aloud the message that was carved into the bark:

"This here tree belongs to none other than Walter Crouly—December 14, 1966, to April 5, 1970."

The leaves rustled in the branches as the wind picked up. Stu closed his eyes and imagined what the next inscription would be:

"The next owner is none other than—"

"Stuart Simmoooons." The ghostly keening of the wind seemed to finish his sentence.

Terrified, Stu whirled around, expecting to see the spirit of Walter Crouly. Instead, he found his father, chuckling mischievously.

"Hell, you almost gave me a heart attack!" he yelled, pretending to throw a punch.

Stephen gathered a handful of leaves, hurled them skyward, and watched them drop back to earth in a delicate, random pattern. "Stu?" he said. "It's gonna take a good while before I can get enough money together to get this place. I'd like to surprise your mom. Think maybe we could keep this whole thing under our hats?"

"I won't tell a soul," Stu said.

They shook hands on it, man to man. For as long as it took, Stu promised himself, he would guard their secret. His father could depend on it.

CHAPTER SEVEN

IN LATE June, many of the farmers needed extra men to harvest potato crops. The wages were low, and the work was back-breaking, but it was there for the asking . . . *if* a fellow was fortunate enough to get hired by the crew foreman. Stephen dug ditches as a soldier and hiked for miles through the jungle under a tropical sun. A month in the potato fields wasn't going to kill him.

The crews were chosen on Monday mornings at dawn. An hour before sunrise, when Stephen showed up in town, there was already a long line of men waiting to be chosen. Most of them were black migrant workers who moved from state to state, following the crops in an endless cycle of poverty. Their clothes were worn, their faces permanently etched with fatigue and resignation. Whatever dreams they might have cherished of bettering their futures had long since faded. They stood unmoving, their shoulders stooped, conserving what little strength they had for the arduous day's work ahead.

Watching the sun come up in a cloudless sky, Stephen spent the next hour brooding about the unfairness of a system that rewarded some men handsomely and robbed others of all hope and opportunity. Compared to the migrants, he was a lucky man. His family had a roof over its head. His kids lived in one place all their lives and ate three meals a day. He owned a truck, and usually, he had enough money to pay for the gasoline.

But he needed work, same as the other men around him. When the farm truck finally arrived at the corner, Stephen squared his shoulders, stood up tall, and prayed he would get picked.

Two men—one white, the other black—got out of the truck and paced the line, pointing at the men whom they wanted to hire. The black man, who was young and powerfully muscled, nodded at Stephen, who jumped into the open back of the truck with the rest of the crew.

By seven o'clock, when Lois and the kids were just waking up, Stephen was squatting in the field, digging potatoes out of the red dirt and dropping them into the burlap sack hung around his neck. The temperature already soared into the nineties, and it didn't take long for Stephen to work up a sweat. He glanced around for the water bucket and noticed the black foreman staring at him.

"You're Lidia's dad, ain't you? I'm Elvadine's half brother, Little Moe," the man said.

"Little Moe?" Stephen grinned. The man had the physique of a football player.

"Think I'm large? You should see Big Moe. Now *he's* big." Little Moe chuckled. Then he said, "Why you out here pickin' spuds?"

"This is the only work I could find," Stephen told him.

"I hear tell they got openings at the mine down the road a piece, in Marbleton. Pays a lot more."

"How come you ain't minin' then?"

Little Moe wiped beads of perspiration off his forehead. "It's a long drive to Marbleton. Besides, it costs twenty-five dollars to get a union card. Where am I gonna get twenty-five dollars from?"

Stephen could have asked him the very same question.

Stu had found a great piece of lumber for one of the side walls of the fort. He was concentrating so hard on dragging it away from the quarry that he didn't notice Ula Lipnicki sneaking up on him until it was too late to escape. She waved to someone behind him. Stu turned and found Ebb blocking his back. Then Ebb whistled, and Arliss and Darla emerged from their hiding places. He was surrounded on three sides by Lipnickis, and the quarry lay in front of him.

"Boy, you do like punishment," said Arliss, moving toward him.

"That's good, 'cuz we like to give it," Ula chimed in.

His choice was simple: stay where he was and get beaten to a pulp or make a break for the ridge. He stared at the muddy quarry waters down below, took a deep breath, and ran for his life. He leaped off the ridge; Arliss and Ebb charging right after him. He hit the water with a thump and churned wildly to the other shore. Then he was off and running again through the woods; his slim lead was enough to save him.

"You can run, chicken boy, but you'll never hide from us," Arliss shouted after him.

With the odds at four to one, Stu decided for once to let him have the last word.

With no one left to torment, the Lipnickis got bored and decided to head for home. "Looky here, I cut my arm!" Leo was saying as they ambled into the yard. "That makes thirty-one scars! I got more than you now."

"Hell you do! I got me more scars than Christ!" Arliss boasted. "Hold your arm up here next to mine!"

They were so caught up in their competition that none of them noticed Lidia and Elvadine cowering with their wagon of loot behind a pile of lumber, where they retreated as soon as they heard Leo's voice.

"Aw, them cigar burns you give yourself don't count. It's gotta be an accident!" Leo scoffed.

"Them cigar burns I'm gonna give that Simmons kid will count double!" said Arliss.

"You can bet on that!" Willard exclaimed.

The girls crouched in their makeshift hiding place, too frightened to move. A few feet away, an old-fashioned man's armoire lay on its side, its doors flung open. Lidia silently pointed it out to Elvadine, who shook her head and whispered, "I can't fit in there."

"Either you hide with me or your butt'll be smoked," Lidia whispered back. But before either of them had a chance to move, she felt a hand on her back. It was Billy, come to save them! His eyes were wide and round with fear as he led them through a patch of uncut grass to the back gate.

"You done good by us, Billy boy," Lidia said quietly, paying him his ten cents. He bobbed his head in thanks. Then he slipped back through the gate and disappeared in the tall grass.

They dashed for the shelter of the woods and stopped running only when they were sure they were far enough away not to be seen. Gasping for breath, they glanced down the path and saw someone walking his bike down the path toward them.

"Uh-oh!" Lidia groaned. Of all the bad luck!

Lester Lucket caught up with them and took a long look at their junk-laden wagon.

"You're gonna be in trouble!" he announced in a singsong tone.

"For what?" snapped Lidia.

"For takin' stuff from the Lipnickis' yard. I'm tellin' right this very second and you can't stop me!" he threatened. "I'd like to see you try!"

"It so happens I got permission."

"I don't believe you, because you would say anythin', because you know I'm gonna tell on you! And when they find out, they're gonna kick your ass!" he sang out in the same irritating tone as before.

Asking Lester Lucket for a favor was just about the lowest, creepiest thing a girl might ever have to do. But she knew he would love nothing more than to tattle on her and Elvadine. "Don't say nuthin', Lester," she pleaded.

"Name me one reason why I shouldn't."

She glanced at Elvadine and sighed, knowing she would regret what she was about to say. "You're going to summer school, aren't you?"

"So?"

"If you keep your big, fat mouth closed, I'll do all your homework," she promised.

Pleased with the bargain, he thumped his chest. "First time I get less than a B, I'm tellin'. Either way, I got you!" he warned. Then he mounted his bike and rode away.

"You know the minute he gets his final grade, he's gonna run like wildfire, straight to the Lipnickis to tattle on us," Elvadine said mournfully.

She wanted to ask Elvadine, if she was so smart, what would *she* have done? But of course, raiding the Lipnickis had been Lidia's idea in the first place, and Elvadine would relish the chance to remind her of that. So all she said was, "Well, that's two months away. Maybe somebody will run him over with a car before then."

Elvadine stared after Lester. "I got me a baaaad feeling about this," she moaned.

She continued her predictions of the dire consequences that awaited them until they got to Lidia's house. Lois told them to hurry and wash up, because supper was almost ready. Elvadine brightened at the mention of food and forgot about Lester and the Lipnickis, at least temporarily.

Stephen called to say he might be late, so Lois decided to feed the children first and wait to eat with him. She asked Elvadine to say grace. Then she passed around heaping portions of salad and fried potatoes.

"How come all we ever eat is potatoes and salad anymore? Baked potatoes, fried potatoes, mashed potatoes!" Lidia complained, wrinkling her nose and pushing away her plate.

"If you ain't hungry, pass it over here, child," Elvadine said between bites of potato.

Lois looked sternly at Lidia, getting ready to remind her how much luckier she was then lots of folks who had nothing to eat for supper. But just then Stephen strolled into the kitchen with Little Moe.

"I got something to tell y'all," he said smiling. "Little Moe and me applied for a job a couple of days ago with the Marbleton Mine Company. We just got word from the foreman sayin' we've been hired."

Lidia bounced up and down in her chair. "Really?" she exclaimed.

Stephen nodded. "Yep. There's only one problem. If we don't show up tomorrow mornin' with a union card, he's gonna give the positions to someone else. Moe here knows how to get the cards, but each card's gonna cost twenty-five dollars, which neither of us has."

"I got three dollars," Lidia said immediately.

"Well, I'd be much obliged if you'd let us borrow it."

"Pay it right back first pay I get, with interest," added Little Moe as Lidia ran to get her money.

Not to be outdone, Stu offered, "I got five and some change."

He fished through his pockets and dropped his contribution onto the table. Lidia raced back into the room with the headless doll that she used for a piggy bank and added her savings to the pot.

Stu started counting. "You got fourteen, Daddy. That's nineteen. Twenty, twenty-one, twenty-two, and ninety-five, a hundred. Twenty-three dollars and fifteen cents."

Lois reached for her purse, took from her wallet three ten-dollar bills, and placed them on top of the pile.

"Mom," said Lidia. "I thought you were savin' that for—"

"A special occasion," Lois broke in, winking at Lidia behind Stephen's back. "And your dad just landed the best job of his life. Congratulations, Stephen." She kissed her husband and patted Moe on the back. "And you too, Moe."

"Now don't you eat them outta house and home, you hear me?" Moe teased Elvadine, who was beaming with happiness.

"We better run now, before the place closes," Stephen said.

"Can I come?" Stu asked Stephen, who nodded. "Sure."

As soon as she heard the door close, Lidia said, "But Mom, that was your book-savings money."

Lois sat down in Stu's chair and picked up a fork to eat his dinner. She took her time responding to Lidia, wondering how best to explain why she had given Stephen the money she had worked so hard to save. Finally, she said, "If your dad knew I was goin' back to school, he might think it's because I didn't believe in him right now."

"Do you?" asked Lidia.

Long ago, Lois decided that one of the hardest parts of being a mother was answering children's questions in a way that was both useful and honest; and the questions got harder as the children got older. There was no easy answer to what Lidia was asking her. Right now, more than anything, the child needed to have faith in her father. Lois would have cut out her tongue rather than weaken that faith.

"I believe he intends to do everything he says," she told Lidia.

Lidia smiled contentedly. Suddenly ravenous, she dug into her food. Her daddy was going to have a great new job, and the fried potatoes were the most delicious thing she had ever eaten.

CHAPTER EIGHT

ON SATURDAY, his first time off since starting at the mine, Stephen announced a "men only" day for himself and Stu. After promising Lidia equal time alone with him the following week, he and Stu packed a couple of sandwiches and took off in the car.

In Vietnam, he dreamed of such days, a chance to be the sort of father his own dad hadn't been. He had seen so much blood and killing there. But he had seen so much beauty, too—the ancient Buddhist temples, the exotic outdoor markets, the lush tropical foliage that tumbled into the ocean—and he yearned to share it all with his children and Lois.

There was beauty close to home, as well. Descending into the mine, he quickly discovered it all around him and wanted Stu to see it, too. He worried that the first trip down might be too disorienting for a child; but Stu reacted as if it were nothing more than a scary carnival ride. Outfitted with a miner's cap like Stephen's, he fell mute with excitement as they boarded the elevator and plunged into almost total darkness.

They stepped off the elevator and onto the

narrow catwalk that jutted out over a large pool of water. A rowboat bobbed gently at the edge of the catwalk. Stephen held it steady so Stu could climb inside, then joined him and pushed off.

He aimed the lantern on his helmet toward the vaulted, white marble ceiling that arched two hundred feet above them. "I do believe this is the most gorgeous sight I've ever seen," he said, speaking in a hushed tone as if they had entered a holy site or place of worship.

Except for an occasional push of the paddle, he let the boat float aimlessly. They drifted into one of the older sections, where the darkness was intermittently pierced by bright patches of sunlight that shone through holes in the side of the mine.

"This here part is abandoned, which is why it's full of water," Stephen explained. He pointed to the narrow, low-ceilinged grottoes carved into the walls. "Look at the caves."

"This is boss," Stu breathed.

The mine had to be the most mysterious, magical place in the world. It was as if he had traveled through space to an alternate universe, where dry land had been replaced by water, and day was night. No wonder his father and Little Moe had so badly wanted those union cards. He couldn't wait to get one, too, as soon as he was old enough.

He could have floated underground for days. But his father had other plans for them. Too soon, Stephen turned the boat around and retraced their route. They now returned to more familiar territory, blinking their eyes to adjust to the sunlight.

"When are you gonna tell me where we're goin'?" Stu asked, as Stephen drove away from the mine.

"It's not a surprise if I tell you," said Stephen.

The last time, his father had surprised him with the house he promised would someday be theirs. What would he come up with this time? Stu kept a sharp eye out for familiar landmarks and soon realized they were driving in the direction of the fairgrounds. But the fair was weeks away. He was totally stumped.

A few minutes later, they passed an enormous sign covered with big black letters that screamed "AUCTION."

"The auction! You're really gonna buy that white house?" he asked incredulously.

Stephen was grinning as he nodded and turned left into the fenced area where the auction was being held. The grounds were crowded with potential customers strolling among the trailers, motor homes, and food stalls whose vendors hawked hot dogs, sweet-potato pie, soda, and beer. All the parking spaces in the nearby field were already filled, and Stephen was searching for a place to park along the boulevard adjacent to the auction site, when Stu suddenly heard a chorus of familiar voices screaming his name.

Those damn Lipnickis! Of all the bad luck!

Four or five of them leered at him from the back of their father's truck. They were munching on watermelon slices and yelling at him as the truck pulled parallel to the Simmons' car.

"Butt face!" Arliss shouted, hurling his rind at Stu.

His aim was deadly. The rind smacked Stu flat on the side of the head. Much to the Lipnickis' delight, a trail of sticky juice and seeds dribbled down his cheek.

"Damn!" Stu swore, feeling in his pocket for a tissue.

Stephen asked, "What happened?"

"They slapped my face with a watermelon."

Stephen handed him his handkerchief. He dabbed at the juice that had squirted in his eye and wiped away the mess on his cheek.

Mr. Lipnicki, meanwhile, switched lanes and pulled in right behind them. Checking his rearview mirror, Stephen saw him weaving across the lane and figured he must be drunk. He sped up to gain some distance, but the effort was too much for his car. The engine first stalled, then died.

"C'mon, Flossy," he coaxed, trying to turn over the engine.

Lipnicki honked his horn loudly as Stephen kept on trying to get the motor started.

"Push that pile of junk to the side of the road!" Lipnicki bellowed.

As if responding to his ill-tempered directive, the car started up. Stephen moved up to the intersection to make a left turn. Flossy died again.

Lipnicki leaned on his horn. The engine sputtered optimistically. Stephen quickly stepped on the gas. But Lipnicki, too impatient to wait, had already begun to edge around him; for one brief second, both vehicles attempted to occupy the same space. The result was two slightly scraped fenders and one screaming, lunatic Lipnicki.

His simmering rage reached its boiling point. He gunned his engine and rammed the truck into the back of the car with such force that it barreled through the intersection.

"Dad!" Stu cried. "He's hittin' our car!"

"I can see that," Stephen said as calmly as he could. He had no interest in fighting with a drunken, screaming maniac. The traffic ahead was stalled, which meant he was stuck for the moment. Experience taught him that the best strategy in such a situation was to keep his mouth shut until the guy either lost interest or sobered up.

Stu, however, wanted vengeance. "Do something!" he urged.

"What do you want me to do, go stand between the bumpers?"

Lipnicki moved forward and bumped the truck again.

Taking matters in his own hands, Stu rolled down the window and sat on the sill. "Hey! Quit hittin' our car, you big fat son-of-a-bitch!" he yelled.

"Hey!" Stephen pulled him back into the truck. "Son, don't do that!"

His warning came too late. Lipnicki charged past the car, skidded into a U-turn, and rocketed backwards until he was window-to-window with Stephen.

"What the hell'd you say to me?" he roared. "That the way you teach your kid, to back-talk adults?"

Stephen tried to keep his voice calm and reasonable. "Well, no. But I think he saw you slammin' against our car like that and got a little emotional . . . besides the fact that your children threw a watermelon upside his head."

"He tricked us into fallin' into a septic tank!" Ula shouted.

"Yeah, I got that dung in my mouth because of him." Willard nodded.

Lipnicki got out of the truck and staggered over to Stu's window.

"You push my kids into a septic?" he spluttered.

Stu flinched as he got a whiff of Lipnicki's sour alcohol breath. "No," he said, ducking his head back into the car.

"Liar, liar, pants on fire, hangin' from a telephone wire!" Willard chanted.

"You lyin' to me, son?" Lipnicki jabbed Stu's chest with a filth-encrusted finger. "You better don't catch yourself lyin' to me."

Stephen decided Lipnicki had gone far enough. He stepped out of the car and walked around to inspect the damage. Stu got out and stood next to him.

"Let's all just let this go. Seems like our kids are gonna live. Doesn't look like there's any damage done to our fine automobiles," he said, still trying to dampen Lipnicki's anger.

Lipnicki sneered. "You bein' smug with me? Huh! 'Cuz if you're itchin' for a fight, I'll give it to you!"

"I'm afraid I don't believe in fightin'."

"Oh, I just bet you don't. Yellow-tailed, chickenshit-ass wussy!" Lipnicki railed.

By now, his kids had scooted over to find front-row seats on the roof of the truck. They hooted loudly as their father shook his fist at Stephen, who didn't even blink.

Stu was raging mad. "Mister, you must be the dumbest scum-bag on this planet to call my dad a wuss!" he yelled.

Lipnicki's face reddened. He clutched Stu by the throat and hissed, "What did you say? I'll break your neck, you little shithead!"

Quick as lightning, Stephen grabbed Lipnicki's arm and twisted it across his shoulder. Then he flipped him onto his back and thrust two fingers over his windpipe. His eyes blazed with anger, but he spoke slowly and quietly. "I'm afraid I can't allow you to put your hands on my son. You don't see me correctin' your children."

Lipnicki gagged and fought for breath. He tried to pull away, but Stephen was too strong for him. He suddenly looked frightened, as if he realized that with very little effort, Stephen could break his neck and kill him if he wanted to.

Stephen leaned in close and eyeballed him. He went on in the same low voice, "I don't mind so much you plowin' into my car. And I don't take offense at you callin' me names. But you go after my child, you're gonna push a button on me, and then I'm gonna lose control and kill you." He took a deep breath, as if to cleanse himself of his fury. Then he asked, "What's your name?"

"Lipnicki," the other man choked out.

Stephen relaxed his grip slightly. "Now apologize to my son."

"I apologize," Lipnicki said, massaging his neck.

"That's mighty kind of you. My son has somethin' to tell you." Stephen turned to Stu. "Apologize to Mr. Lipnicki, Stu. Tell him you're sorry for insultin' him."

Lipnicki's mouth went slack as he quite obviously pondered what the hell this guy was up to.

Bewildered and mortified by what felt like a double cross, Stu glared at his father. "Sorry, Mr. Lipnicki."

The incident handled, Stephen released Lipnicki, who stumbled back to his truck. "You near busted my windpipe. This ain't over! No little son-of-a-bitch is gonna push my kids into a sewer hole and dance away like he done nuthin'!" he shrieked.

"Burn rubber, Dad!" cried Ebb, hopping down from the roof.

"Get the hell out, all of you!" Lipnicki roared at his brood.

"What'd we do?" demanded Leo.

Lipnicki's fist shot out. It connected with Leo's jaw with such force that the boy was almost knocked to the ground. Then he jumped into the cab of the truck and zoomed away, leaving his children to find their own way home.

Leo glared at Stu, and Arliss flipped him the

finger as a parting gesture. Then he sauntered off with his brothers and sisters, who seemed to accept their father's abrupt departure as a perfectly natural turn of events.

"I'm sorry you had to witness that," Stephen said, once he and Stu were back in the car. "I try to show you the right ways and then I almost lose my control again and hurt someone."

Stu felt close to crying from having been humiliated in front of his sworn enemies. "But he called you names. Banged our car up," he muttered.

"Man's got problems, Stu. Did more damage to his own truck than he did to Flossy." Stephen turned the ignition key, and the car started up without so much as a cough. "Lookit that, purrin' like a kitten. . . . I think everybody likes to get banged once in awhile."

In spite of himself, Stu cracked up laughing and instantly forgave his father.

"Don't tell your mom I said that," said Stephen with a conspiratorial smile.

Stu grinned and watched Stephen maneuver through the traffic until he found a place to park. His dad was absolutely the greatest guy ever, he decided, as they strolled through the crowd of people, many of whom were munching on popcorn and cotton candy.

Finally, they reached the registration table, which was strewn with sheets of information. One of the auction clerks, a heavyset man sporting a cowboy hat and a bolo tie, greeted them heartily.

"Howdy, neighbor. What can I do for you?" he asked Stephen.

Stephen showed him the auction advertisement he had torn out of the newspaper. "How would we go about making a bid on this piece of property?"

"Well, sir, the houses are being sold through what they call blind bids. What you do is make out a personal check for the highest amount you're willin' to pay," he explained. He nodded at a large wooden box with a narrow slit at the top, secured by a padlock, that sat in the middle of the table. "We'll give you a call in the next few days if you win."

Stephen carefully wrote out a check and stuffed it into an envelope. "You wanna kiss it for added luck?" he asked Stu.

Stu licked the envelope, and they *both* kissed it for luck. Then Stu shoved it through the opening in the box.

"There's no minimum bid?" Stephen asked hopefully.

"There isn't, but we try not to encourage the cheapskates. Some folks were writing out checks for a nickel and causing us real headaches."

"Well, my check isn't anywhere near five thousand dollars," said Stephen, naming the figure that he thought the house was worth. "You reckon I'd still have a chance?"

"Probably not. You ever consider maybe purchasing a mobile home?" The clerk pointed to the row of them lined up behind the registration table. "Every trailer house you see here today starts off at one penny."

"Where do they end up?"

"Usually around fifteen hundred or so," the clerk said.

Stephen looked so shocked that Stu figured he had to say something to cheer him up. Though the mobile homes seemed hardly any improvement over the shack they were living in now, he said, "Nothin' wrong with startin' small and workin' up."

"I really like the white house the best," Stephen said, trying to hide his disappointment. "If we don't get it, we'll come back again when we have more cash. Next month, how about?"

Stu shrugged. "Sure. Why not?" He remembered his teacher telling them about a Spanish guy named Don Quixote and his impossible dream. That's all the beautiful white house was—an impossible dream that could never be theirs. But if his dad needed to hang onto that dream—if it helped him feel better—Stu wasn't about to burst his bubble.

"What do you say we go get your mom and your sister some cotton candy?" Stephen suggested, putting his arm around Stu's shoulder as they walked toward the vendors. Suddenly, Stu felt himself being enveloped by the throng and realized he had been separated from his father.

"Dad?" he called. Stephen had vanished. He continued searching through the swarm of eager bidders until he realized he had walked all the way to the main entrance of the fairgrounds. His father was still nowhere in sight. But to his chagrin, he found four of the Lipnickis hanging out on the steps of one of the auction trailers, panhandling and harassing passersby.

"Mister, can you spare a dollar so me and my brothers could get somethin' to eat?" Arliss hailed an old man, who hobbled past leaning heavily on his cane. When the man didn't so much as glance his way, Arliss yelled after him, "You bald-headed son-of-a-bitch!"

Stu turned aside quickly, trying to skirt around the back of the trailer before they spotted him. But he wasn't quick enough for Willard, who bounded down the steps and stepped in front of him.

"Hey, punk! Don't you know you can't buy no houses with food stamps?" Willard gibed.

Stu thought about his father and not losing control. He clamped his lips together to keep from answering and tried to sidestep Willard to get to the exit. But Ebb blocked his way, saying, "No, Willard, his daddy has a job. Remember we seen him? Pluckin' spuds out in the field!"

Stu took a deep breath and clenched his fists.

"Then again," Ebb continued loudly, "maybe he was just thievin' them potatoes for supper!"

Disrespectful of his dad by calling him a thief was more than Stu could take from this bunch of mealy-mouthed bullies. He lunged at Ebb and tried to hit him; his aim was off. Ebb's was better; his swift kick got Stu squarely in the groin. He moaned and doubled over in pain. Willard immediately jumped in and started throwing punches. Stu lashed back at him, and then both boys were rolling in the dirt, their fists flying at each other.

By now, Leo and Arliss had joined in the fray, hollering instructions at Willard and making the most of every opportunity to kick Stu.

It would have been a rout if Stephen hadn't caught up with him just then. He rushed over and pulled Willard off Stu's back.

"Go on!" he shouted at the others, who had gathered around Willard to congratulate him. "Get on with your business!" he shouted again. Savoring their win, they finally meandered away.

Stu dusted himself off and faced his father, who was still carrying two cones of cotton candy.

"I guess this is all my fault," Stephen said sadly. "If I can't control myself, how do I expect you to?"

Stu wished he could make his father understand. "It ain't your fault. I hate them kids!"

They walked in silence toward the car. Then, as if he hadn't had his fill of Lipnickis, Stu saw Ula and Darla playing in the dirt under a tree.

"Hey, trespasser! I know a house your daddy can afford," Ula announced. She pointed up to the branches and giggled. "'Course a couple of robins are livin' in it now."

"Shut up, dogface!" Stu screamed.

"Get in the car, son," Stephen said quietly.

Stu wished the Lipnickis would get sucked up by an earthquake and disappear forever. He stormed off to the car, expecting his father to follow. He was stunned when he looked around to see that Stephen had walked up to the two girls and was calmly handing each of them a cotton candy.

"I hope you know," Stu grumpily announced

when his father finally rejoined him, "their brothers are the ones just beat me up."

Stephen nodded. "I know who they are, son."

"Then why'd you just give them Mom and Lidia's cotton candy?"

"Because they look like they hadn't been given anythin' in a long time," Stephen said evenly.

Stu's lip was beginning to swell, and his right cheek throbbed with the bruises he knew would soon begin to show. He knew what *he* would have given them—the punch in the face they deserved. But he figured he'd better keep his ideas to himself, at least until his father realized what snakes the Lipnickis really were. He seethed in silence while his father drove him over to the fort.

By the time they got there, he felt so confused he didn't know whether he was angrier at the Lipnickis or his father, who seemed unaware of his feelings.

"You're doin' a beautiful job on that. Where you findin' all that stuff?" asked Stephen, inspecting the nearly completed structure. The foundation had been completely laid down, and the boys had hung tarps to create a temporary roof and walls.

"I don't know." Stu kicked at an empty soda bottle that one of them had left behind. "Lidia gets it."

"Stu?" Stephen hunkered down on a pile of lumber and motioned for Stu to join him.

Stu kept on kicking at the bottle.

Stephen sighed. The boy deserved some kind of explanation. He said, "Son? Those kids are dirt poor. They probably don't get enough to eat. Their daddy beats them, they don't even have a mamma. Now, I'm not sayin' that gives them the right to cut you down, but it's not gonna do you any good to kill each other. Have you tried talkin' to them?"

Stu whirled around and glared at his father. "They ain't got a reason to bully me. Talkin' to them ain't gonna give them a reason not to."

His wounded face was a study in hurt and confusion. Stephen only hoped he could find the right words to make him understand.

"Maybe all they know is fightin'. I guess that's all the world ever taught them."

"They were sayin' horrible things about us. You wouldn't stand by and just let somebody dog Mom, would you?" Stu asked as he picked up the bottle and sent it flying into a thicket of trees.

"No. I wouldn't. If they start pushin' you around, of course you gotta defend yourself. I'm just sayin' it'd be better if you could avoid tanglin' as much as possible."

"It's self-defense, Dad. You went to war, to fight for people you didn't even know," Stu pointedly reminded him.

"Yes, I did," he said. And what a terrible price he paid for his simpleminded act of patriotism. He motioned to Stu to come sit next to him. Then he went on, "I wanted to help people. But in the end, I killed more than I saved. I lost more friends than I've ever made, before or since. I lost my dignity, I lost my house, and I nearly lost my family."

Bewildered, Stu said what he knew to be the truth. "You're a hero."

Stephen sighed. "Stu, I think it's time I tell you why I've been havin' those nightmares. Did I ever tell you about my friend, Dodge?"

"Uh-uh," Stu said eagerly.

"We went through boot camp together and we swore we'd stick by one another, come what may. But after trainin', we were sent on different missions and split up," Stephen began, hoping he was doing the right thing by leading his son into the terrible place and time he had tried so hard to forget.

"I lived in a tree and hunted. I hunted people. I killed them with my rifle. And sometimes, I even killed with my own hands. I hid in tunnels and I saw things that made my skin crawl. Women and children killed like farm animals by their own kind and by my kind. After awhile, I could hardly talk."

He could feel, without a word being spoken between them, that Stu was right there with him, soaking up every word, straining to make sense of matters he hardly understood himself. "Then I met up with Dodge again. He helped me calm down a bit, so I wasn't so cut up inside. I started to talk again and almost felt human. I think his kindness hurt more than some of those wounds I received." A sob caught in his throat as he said, "You sure you wanna hear this, Stu?"

"Yes, sir." Stu nodded.

"One day, we were on patrol and there was a fire fight. A grenade landed only a few feet from me. Dodge saw it and knocked me into a ditch as it went off. When I got up, he was near sawed in half. I tried to breathe life into him, but nothin' happened. I carried him to the chopper, but they said he was dead. They pulled me off him, and the next thing I knew I was in the chopper, lookin' down on Dodge as he started to crawl through the grass when machine-gun fire strafed his body. I had left him alive. Two days later, my country presented me with a Purple Heart and a Bronze Star for bravery."

Fearful of seeing reflected in Stu's eyes the contempt he had lived with every day since then, he, nevertheless, forced himself to look at Stu.

"You *are* a hero," Stu insisted, weeping openly. "You didn't do nothin' wrong, Dad."

"That's what my nightmare has been about for two years," Stephen continued, almost as if he hadn't heard what Stu said. "To forgive myself. To pardon my country. I can't tell you never to fight. But if you want to know what I think, I think the only thing that truly keeps people safe and happy is love. I think that's where men find their courage. That's where countries get their strength. And that's where God grants us miracles. And in the absence of love, there's nothin' in this world worth fightin' for."

Stu struggled to follow everything his dad was telling him. Not all of it made sense; how could his father not forgive himself for what was so obviously not his fault? The part about God's miracles he would have to think more about, later, when he was all alone. And he honestly didn't think he could ever love the Lipnickis.

But he wanted to give his father something in

return, to show him that he understood. So he promised, "I'll try to work it out with the Lipnickis."

"I know you will. My life won't amount to much, so all of my hopes rest on you. If you weren't born for a higher purpose than me, then I can't figure out why the good Lord put me on this earth." Stephen put his arms around Stu and hugged him tightly. "I love you, boy," he said.

"I love you, too, Dad," said Stu.

CHAPTER NINE

WATCHING STU take out his frustration on the empty soda bottle gave Stephen an idea. He left Stu at the fort and returned to the mine, where he spent the next couple of hours doing unpaid volunteer cleanup duty. Some men brought their wives gifts of flowers or candies. Stephen figured that what he was bringing home to Lois would please her a whole lot more than any box of chocolates he could ever afford.

When he pulled up in front of the house, he saw her head bent over the sink, framed by the open window. "Honey," he called as he got out of the car. "Would you do me a big favor and come out here?"

Exhaustion was etched on her face as she came out to greet him, drying her hands on her apron. He kissed her, opened the hood of the trunk, and stood back to watch her reaction. Lois shook her head and laughed softly when she saw what he had collected there. The lines of fatigue around her mouth and eyes seemed to soften and fade. She didn't say a word, but she didn't have to. The love and gratitude that showed in her eyes were all the thanks he needed.

"That mine is so littered with bottles," he said,

as she gaped at the hundreds he had brought for her to redeem. "I thought I'd do the company a favor and collect them and throw them away. Less you want them for somethin'."

Lois smiled and stood on her tiptoes to nuzzle his neck, in the same special way he remembered her doing it before the kids were born. "That Lidia, huh?"

"Keepin' secrets is not one of her strong points," he said, holding her hand.

Mrs. Higgens's door slammed, and they smiled at each other, knowing that any second she would be loudly minding their business. Stephen couldn't have cared less. The old biddy could carry on all she wanted. With Lois' arms wrapped around him and her head resting in the crook of his neck, he was sure the good Lord granted him the miracle of love he had been telling Stu about. Maybe one day soon he might even be able to make peace with himself about Dodge.

The day after the auction, Stu was poking around in the cluttered storage hut behind their house for extra tools and accidentally stumbled on his father's army footlocker. He pulled open the cover and found inside a treasure trove of souvenirs from Stephen's career as a soldier.

The trunk had not been locked, but for no reason he could name, he suspected he wasn't supposed to be going through it. Glancing over his shoulder to check that no one was coming, he sifted through the jumble of items. There was a picture of his father, snappily outfitted in his army uniform, solemnly staring at the camera. A second photograph showed Stephen—this time dressed in a T-shirt, shorts, and his dog tags—cutting the hair of another young soldier, whom Stu recognized as Dodge. Sure enough, on the back were the words, "Me and Dodge. May, 1968."

He put the pictures back inside the trunk and took out a small box covered in dark red velvet that felt heavy and important in his hand. He raised the lid and felt his heart beating faster than usual. *His father's medals!*

He removed them from their satiny bed and ran his fingers over the inscriptions. They gleamed faintly in the gloomy light. He closed his eyes and imagined them in the sunlight, polished and hanging from his father's uniformed chest.

Suddenly, the top of the footlocker slammed shut. Stu jumped, expecting to hear an admonishing voice behind him. False alarm—it was only a brisk gust of wind that whistled through the shack, rustling the leaves strewn across the floor. Nevertheless, he opened the locker and quickly returned everything to its place.

He picked up the old-fashioned padlock that lay on the floor next to the trunk, stuck it through the latch, and twisted the key. He thought again about the medals, how they had felt under his fingers, their beauty and weight. Anyone could unlock the trunk and steal the little velvet box that held the official evidence of his father's courage. He couldn't let that happen. He unlocked the trunk, removed the medals, and shoved them into his pocket. He would bring them to the fort—for safekeeping.

Summer school had become a living hell for Lidia. Every morning, she felt as if she and Elvadine were chewing their legs off, like a couple of tortured animals, trying to get away from The Trap, otherwise known as Miss Strapford.

Even worse was the trap Lidia had created for herself with Lester Lucket. Miss Strapford loved assigning compositions, so Lidia was kept busy writing her own papers as well as Lester's. She came to dread the moment when Miss Strapford would announce, "I thought we'd do some writing this morning, class. Won't that be fun?"

No. It was definitely not fun to be biting her fingernails, rushing to finish her paper so she would have time to write one for Lester. She despised him more each day, most especially when he would pretend to thank her by puckering his big ugly lips, pretending to send her a kiss.

Imagine getting kissed by Lester Lucket! The very thought made her want to puke. Yet here she was, doing his schoolwork, earning him B's. And all because he caught her taking from the Lipnickis what actually belonged to her and her family.

She chewed her fingernails, considered the mess she had gotten herself into, and wondered how it was that life could be so terribly unfair.

Ambertree celebrated the Fourth of July with a parade at noon, fireworks after sunset, and afternoon-long family picnics. The children of Ambertree had another reason to celebrate the Fourth. It marked the first summer day that the ice-cream man filled the freezer section of his truck with all sorts of delicious concoctions and took to the streets with his wares.

Billy Lipnicki had been daydreaming about the ice-cream man for almost a year now, ever since last summer when Ula, in an uncharacteristic fit of generosity, bought him his first and only chocolate pop. In all his five years, he never experienced anything quite as wonderful as the hard chocolate crust studded with peanuts that melted in his mouth to reveal a block of deliciously sweet vanilla ice cream wrapped around a stick.

Thanks to Lidia and Elvadine, Billy amassed a large pile of dimes, which he kept hidden under a brick in what once was his mother's vegetable garden. He remembered the bell that had signaled the arrival of the ice-cream man. He hoarded his money, impatiently awaiting the day he would hear that bell again.

He could have asked one of his brothers or sisters when the ice-cream man was coming. But they would have said, why did he care? Where would he get the money to buy himself an ice-cream pop? And then they might have discovered his buried treasure in the garden and stolen every last cent of it away from him.

Instead, he listened hopefully every afternoon. Finally, on the Fourth of July, when the rest of the Lipnickis had walked into town to watch the parade, he heard the bell ringing in the distance.

He ran and grabbed his dimes, his entire fortune, and raced out to the street, thereby becoming the ice-cream man's very first customer of the summer.

The ice-cream man figured the little tow-headed boy with the fistful of dimes had been sent to buy treats for his whole family. Billy kept pointing to the pictures of the pops, bars, and sandwiches that were painted on the side of the truck and handing over his dimes as fast as the ice-cream man could pull the items from the freezer.

He carried them all home in a bag and settled himself on his back stoop to feast. The first three—nut-covered vanilla pops—were every bit as yummy as he had recalled. The fourth, a layer of chocolate ice cream sandwiched between two soft chocolate wafers, was also very tasty, but seemed to make his stomach ache just a bit. The next three, all-chocolate fudge bars, were so sweet they made his tongue curl.

Rebel, his big old yellow dog, was sniffing around, begging for a treat. Billy unwrapped a couple of fudge bars for him. He was beginning to get a headache now from biting into so much cold. His stomachache was getting worse, and he had a funny sensation in his throat, like the time he'd had a temperature and had to throw up in the toilet. He wished he could save what was left to eat later. But the ice cream would melt quickly on such a hot day, and he had waited too long to waste any of it. Maybe, though, he could take a nap, just for a minute.

He put his head down on the stoop and slept,

while Rebel lapped up most of the leftovers. Billy's father found him there a while later, sprawled half-conscious in the dirt, surrounded by a dozen ice-cream wrappers and a puddle of melted ice cream oozing off the sticks. Drunk though he was, John Lipnicki could see his youngest wasn't looking very well.

"Goddangit!" he shouted for the older children. "Arliss, Leo, Willard! Get your good-for-nothin' carcasses over here!"

The bunch of them, just coming back from the parade, heard him cursing and screaming all the way down the street.

"What the hell does he want now?" grumbled Arliss.

"I told you we shouldn't have come home," Leo said.

John Lipnicki stood on the porch, swigging beer out of a long-necked bottle. "Look at him! He can't even get up!" he gestured with the bottle.

"What's the matter with him?" Arliss asked.

"You tell me!"

Arliss picked up one of the ice-cream wrappers and shrugged. "I don't know. Ice cream coma?"

"He's your goddang brother, for cryin' out loud. How many times I have to tell y'all to keep an eye on him? Your mamma, may she rest in peace, would damn me to hell if anythin' ever happened to him."

John Lipnicki slammed the bottom of the bottle between Arliss' shoulder blades for emphasis and added, "I ought to beat every last one of you for lettin' him waller in the dirt. He's just five years old! Now get him cleaned up before the ants carry him off. And from now on, any of you leave this yard without him, it's gonna be on a stretcher!"

He lurched into the house to fetch himself another beer. As soon as he was gone, Leo hauled Billy to his feet. "Get up! You almost got my ears tore off, you stupid idiot!" he said.

Willard counted the ice-cream wrappers on the ground and stared at his brother, who looked pale and wobbly. "Where'd you get all that, anyhow?" he demanded.

"A big airplane just dropped them outta the sky," Billy said, wishing he could go curl up on his bed.

"You don't honest up, Billy, we're gonna scrub you with lipstick so everyone will think you got diaper rash," Willard threatened.

"Nu-uh," whimpered Billy. Of all his brothers, he feared Willard the most. He wasn't the oldest, but he was certainly the meanest, and he always made good on his threats.

"Yeah," Arliss put in. "And after that, we gonna shave your head bald as a witch's tit."

"I ain't gonna look like no witch's tits!" Billy cried.

"Yes, you will, if you don't hurry up and tell us," said Arliss.

Billy stuck out his bottom lip and looked from Arliss to Willard. Those girls with the dimes always treated him nicely, never called him names, never hit or pinched him. If he tattled on them, he would get them in trouble, and himself as well.

"Well, you could cut out every hair on my head.

I ain't tellin' you ding-dittly-ding dang dong!" he said, and took off at a run.

It took a few days for Stu's bruises from his latest encounter with the Lipnickis to ripen. Chet and Marsh didn't seem to notice as the three of them worked together to put the finishing touches on the fort. By the time they threw up the walls and ceiling, hammered in the last nail, and moved in all the furniture the girls had been turning up, the place looked terrific beyond anything they could have anticipated.

The boys had loudly objected, but at Lidia's insistence (and she was, after all, the boss), they painted the walls hot pink. Chet put up an army recruiting poster on one wall, so that a picture of Uncle Sam peered at them beneath the words, "I want you for the U.S. Army." It seemed appropriate, somehow, especially because Stephen's army lock and key hung from the hook that secured the door from the inside.

The rusty old wood-burning stove Lidia and Elvadine had taken from the Lipnickis sat in the middle of the floor, with its pipe protruding through a hole in the corrugated tin roof. Next to it was a wooden rocking horse. Also arranged around the room were teetery straw lounge chairs, a sagging cot, and fruit crates covered with yellowing magazines and comic books. A staircase led up to the boys' favorite spot, the lookout tower on the second floor, which provided an excellent view of the surrounding ridges, as well as the foot paths twenty-five feet below that led to the fort.

Everyone was so pleased with the results that a truce had been declared between the boys and the girls, at least temporarily. On this, the first day that there was nothing left to do, they were all peacefully coexisting. Elvadine's radio was tuned to a Motown station for background music while she and the other girls played jacks. Chet and Marsh were smoking cigarettes and drinking the beers Marsh had sneaked out of his house while they waited for Stu to arrive so they could start their poker game.

"Jesus, man!" Marsh exclaimed, when Stu opened the door. He pointed to the angry red shiner that had ripened around Stu's left eye. "What the hell happened to you? Don't you get tired of them creamin' your ass?"

Marsh was totally predictable. Stu had prepared himself for one of his wise guy comments. "Not really. I kind of enjoy it," he said, winking at Chet as he searched the room for a good place to hide his dad's medals. He found the perfect spot behind a pile of wood that had been stacked against the far wall.

"I wouldn't take that crap from no one," Marsh was saying as he anted up the bottle caps they were using for chips.

Elvadine, walking past him to leave the fort, rolled her eyes, and Chet hooted, "Yeah? I didn't see you doin' much when they had you folded up like a pretzel. You in?" he asked Stu.

Stu nodded and fastened the lock in the latch after Elvadine. Chet dealt him a hand from his nudie deck, and they started the game.

"I told you," said Marsh. "I was takin' the heat for you Maryannes! Seriously, Stu, with guys like them, you gotta kick ass and take no prisoners."

"My dad prefers me not to fight," said Stu, fanning his cards.

"Jesus! Do you do everythin' your old man tells you? Simmons, you ever considered maybe he tells you not to fight 'cause he's a pussy?"

Stu glowered at Marsh, who realized he had gone too far. "Just throwin' out a thought, man," he said quickly. "Don't get a boner!"

Chet jumped in to defend Stu's honor and smooth over the crisis. "You're such an asshole, Marsh! Shit, if anyone's old man's brave, it's Stu's. He was the only dog in his unit to make it out of the war alive. Carried a Joe ten miles with a grenade in his gut. If that ain't some heroic shit, I don't know what is. I bet he tells you cool stories about the war."

Stu squirmed as Chet repeated the story Stu had concocted from whatever scraps of information he had been able to pry loose from his mother. The truth, as told to him by his father, was painfully different from his made-up version.

"He doesn't talk about that stuff too much," he said in a low voice.

Their discussion was interrupted by a sharp knock at the door.

"Password?" called Chet.

"The Lipnickis are comin'!" came Elvadine's urgent response.

Stu unfastened the latch, and Elvadine scurried through the door. She joined the other five kids at the window, where they could see the Lipnickis crossing the meadow that lay between the fort and the ridge.

"They got the quarry. What the hell they doin' here?" Stu griped. "You guys tell them about this place?"

"Of course not," said Chet.

"No way, man," Marsh assured him.

The girls exchanged nervous glances. Elvadine knew she shouldn't have gone along with Lidia's harebrained ideas. Now the chickens were coming home to roost, and she wanted to be well clear of the barn before they arrived.

"Well, I gotta go home. My mamma gotta do my hair," she said.

"See you, Lidia," said Amber, hurrying after her.

The door swung shut behind them, leaving Lidia to wonder whatever happened to loyalty. She couldn't believe her two friends—and Elvadine, especially—had deserted her. And maybe they were jumping to conclusions about the Lipnickis, who weren't necessarily headed for the fort just because they were walking in their direction.

She looked out the window again and saw Willard gesturing toward the fort. Could Billy have squealed on them? Why had she trusted him? He was just a little kid, and he was, after all, a Lipnicki. She groaned, thinking of all the dimes she had wasted on him.

She knew she should tell Stu; he would figure out a solution, the way he always did. But her mouth had gone dry, and her tongue was refusing to take orders from her brain.

"What?" Stu said, noticing the guilty look on her face.

"I was gonna tell you," she began, and then her nerve failed her.

"Tell me what? What'd you do, Lidia?"

"You're not gonna be mad at me or anythin', are you?" she begged. "I didn't steal all of it. Their old man took a lot of it from our old house."

"Oh, man! I warned you, Stu! A walkin', talkin' broadcast station, that's what she is! That's it, man, I fold!" Marsh announced.

He was gone before Stu could say a word.

"They're halfway across the lot!" Chet reported from his post at the window. "What are we doin'?"

"Go out and stall them a minute. I gotta think," Stu told him.

Chet slipped out the door, leaving Stu alone with his sister. She hung her head, preparing herself for the punishment she knew she deserved. Stu thought about the stove, the torn-up lawn chairs, the ratty blankets, and all the rest of the stuff Lidia had hauled to the fort day after day.

The picture came to him in a flash. It wasn't pretty. He could have kicked himself for not getting it sooner. His sister was a menace—to herself, to him, to his friends.

He threw up his hands in disgust. As usual, he now had to figure out how to save the day; except, this time, Lidia had truly outdone herself in stupidity.

She read his mind. "I admit it," she shame-facedly offered. "I shouldn't have been there."

"Yeah," he said.

"I screwed up."

"Yeah," he prompted her.

She told him she was sorry. There was nothing more she could say except, "All right. Let's not make a big thing out of this. So now what?"

He reviewed the various options; none of them added up to an answer. "I don't know," he said honestly.

"Stu!" Chet called to him. "It's kind of important you come out here now."

Stu turned to go down the ladder, but Lidia grabbed his arm. "You're not thinkin' of handin' it all back?" she demanded. "This is our house. Maybe the only one we're gonna ever really have, and it's our stuff in the first place. Don't you think we ought to fight for it?"

"Oh, Stu!" Chet shouting, trying to keep the panic out of his voice. "Your guests have arrived."

"Don't you recall a damn thing Daddy's taught us?" Stu said furiously. "He finds out we been fightin' again and he's gonna be real disappointed!"

Lidia knew he was right, which only made her feel a hundred times worse. "We'll figure another way, that's all," Lidia said, trying to sound as if she meant it. "No fightin'."

Stu thought about the promise he made his father to try and work things out with the Lipnickis. He pulled out of her grasp and started down the ladder to face them.

"We'll just let them kill us if we have to," said Lidia, coming down after him.

He could have slapped her for making jokes and leaving him to handle the crisis. Any fool could tell immediately that this was no joking matter. Elvadine, Amber, Chet, and Marsh were huddled in a circle, surrounded by all the Lipnicki kids except Billy, who stood off to the side. Willard and Arliss had Elvadine pinned against a tree. Her arms were crossed against her chest, and she was crying.

"What happened?" Stu asked.

Chet said, "They gave her a titty twister."

The Lipnickis seemed to think that was the funniest thing they had ever heard.

"I never done nothin' to you!" Elvadine yelled at her tormentors.

They cracked up again. "Now do the other one," Arliss told Willard.

"Leave her alone!" shouted Stu.

Willard grabbed for Elvadine's breast, but she twisted sideways and kicked him in the groin. "I'm gonna tell my big brother and he's gonna kick all your asses!" she sobbed. "'Cause I never once done nothin' to you!"

"You get your filthy nigger feet off of my brother, bitch!" yelled Arliss.

Lidia wanted to rip his head off for hurting Elvadine and calling her names. Too angry to think, she threw herself at him, her fists flying.

Stu acted quickly. He jumped in between them and said, "Leave Elvadine alone. She's just a girl.

She's got enough problems without you all tweakin' her titties."

Arliss guffawed, and that got the rest of his brothers laughing, too. Stu hadn't meant to amuse them, but if he could give them a good yuck and break the tension, what the hell?

Their attention diverted from Elvadine, the Lipnickis trooped up the ladder, followed by Stu and Lidia. Stu could tell from Arliss' expression that he was impressed by the elaborate accommodations. He jumped up and down, as if to check the solidity of the construction.

Willard examined Stu's lock and key. "Bitchen lock. Where'd you get it?" he asked.

"It's my dad's. It came from the war. You can play with it if you like," Stu offered.

"Goody gumdrops. I think I'll just take it on home and play with it," Willard said sarcastically. He removed the lock from the door and shoved it in his pocket.

Before Stu had a chance to protest, Leo yelped, "That there's our stove, I'll tell you that right now."

Stu threw Lidia a warning glance, but there was no stopping her. "Well, your dad stole all the leftover stuff from our house!" she burst out.

"That stuff was just junk!" said Arliss.

"It was our junk!"

"It wasn't your junk after the city repossessed it."

"Well, it wasn't your junk neither!" Lidia shot back.

"Hell, you don't need to claim this junk," said

140

Stu, trying to make peace. "You can come visit any time you like."

"Yeah!" Billy said enthusiastically.

"Shut up, Billy! You little dip!" Arliss yelled and grabbed Stu by the front of his shirt. He pushed him up against the wall and spat out a big slobbering gob of saliva that hit Stu square in his eye.

"You got five seconds to tell me an idea I like better than seizin' this here place for our own," he snarled, as the saliva dripped down Stu's cheek. "Four, three, two—"

"We'll dare you for it," Lidia said.

"All right!" said Leo. "Cool, Arliss! A dare."

Arliss looked at Lidia. "What kind of dare?"

"Any kind you say. But if we win, we keep the fort."

"And if you lose?"

"It's yours. Lock and key," Lidia said, glancing at Stu, as if to say, what choice do we have?

They were in for it now. There was no telling what the Lipnickis might come up with.

Arliss let go of Stu and grinned at Lidia. "Fine by us."

CHAPTER TEN

ARLISS DIDN'T waste a second choosing the dare. Stu and his friends shuddered when he set out the terms. Short of lying down on the tracks to wait for a train, no stunt was more dangerous than the one he was proposing. Each side was to pick someone to swim the water tower. It sounded simple when he said it. But even Marsh, who liked to pretend nothing fazed him, turned pale at the thought.

They had all been warned by their parents to stay away from the massive water tower, which loomed on the horizon for miles around. "That's no place to play!" their mothers had drummed in to them from the time they were old enough to go off on their own. In the early part of the century, before a proper modern reservoir had been built, the tower held the town's water supply. By now, however, it had disintegrated into a decrepit old eyesore that everyone agreed should be torn down, yet never was.

The tower was surrounded by a high barbed-wire fence, posted with "Danger! No trespassing!" signs. Yet every spring, there were always those high-school seniors who felt it their duty to leave their mark on the tower. It didn't matter how many local cops were assigned to patrol the area. The seniors somehow managed to get past the fence, climb the rusted iron ladder on the outside of the tank, and paint over the faded message left by their predecessors.

That no one had ever been killed there was generally considered nothing short of a miracle. Years earlier, according to local legend, a beautiful young woman who had been spurned by the man she adored had drowned herself in the tower. Though Lois had scoffed at the story when the twins repeated it to her, Lidia believed it was true. It thrilled her to imagine the young woman, who was said to have had long black hair that trailed down her back, standing at the top of the tower, preparing to jump rather than face life without the man she loved.

She never thought of climbing the tower herself, however, and thinking about it now sent shivers up her spine. She could tell that Stu didn't much like the idea either. But a dare was a dare. Backing down now would mean not only losing the fort, but being branded sissies and cowards by the Lipnickis. The shame would be too much to bear.

Stu stared up at the tower. The side facing him was inscribed with a crude drawing of a skull and crossbones, with the words "The Devil's Womb" scrawled underneath. Stu didn't believe that the mythical young woman—or anyone else, for that matter—had drowned in the tower. But he wasn't eager to swim the pool of water himself, even if Arliss claimed to have done it dozens of times.

He knew, though, that he would have to be the one to represent his side; as the two groups slipped through a tear in the fence, in his head, he listed the reasons why. For one thing, he was the strongest swimmer of all his friends. Secondly, the dare had been Lidia's idea, and like it or not, she was his sister. But most important, he was determined to prove to his father that he could find a way other than fighting to settle his beef with the Lipnickis.

"If we win the key, do we get to own the fort and say who's in it?" asked Billy, as they came up to the tower.

"Yeah, Billy boy," Willard said, tossing the lock and key in the air. "That's what we get to do."

"If I get the key, I'd have it be everyone's," Billy said.

Stu smiled at Billy. Somebody who didn't know much about barbering had shaved off large clumps of his hair. But even with his godawful haircut, the kid was pretty cute, for a Lipnicki.

Arliss whacked his little brother in the back of the head. "Shut up, you little broken record," he said.

He started up the ladder, with the rest of the kids following him. Halfway up the facade, Marsh made the mistake of looking back and almost lost his lunch. "Sweet Jesus!" he exclaimed.

Just then, the wind picked up, blowing harshly in their faces and rattling the ladder. Billy, who was sandwiched between Leo and Willard, lost his footing and began to slide off the rung.

"Willard! Grab him!" Leo yelled.

"Hold on, asshole!" Willard shouted at Billy, grabbing hold of him.

"I am holdin' on!" Billy said, wishing now that he had stayed at home.

"Who the hell's supposed to be watchin' him anyways?" Arliss demanded. "Ula?"

Ula glared at her brother, several rungs above her. "Excuse me very much, but I am!"

They continued upwards, slowly proceeding to the top of the tower like ants crawling up a mountainside. It seemed like an eternity until they reached the summit. When Stu stepped off the final rung of the ladder and saw what lay ahead, he gulped. Stretched across the top of the tower was a platform of rotten planks. Many of the planks had already collapsed, leaving huge gaping holes in the surface.

Approximately midway across the platform was a second ladder that led down into the interior of the tank. With the seeming ease of seasoned trapeze artists, the Lipnickis hopped from one board to the next toward the ladder. Stu made his way more cautiously, half-stooping, half-crawling across the boards. He could hear Lidia, right behind him, grunting with the effort of keeping her balance.

He stopped to catch his breath and peered through a crevice into the darkness. Lidia crawled over and stretched out next to him. Earlier, climbing the tower, Stu wondered whether the pool was eerily calm and beautiful, like the section of the mine he had explored with his father. Now he had his answer, as strange, horrible sounds echoed up at them, the belches and gurgles of a race of giants.

Lidia pulled out her cigarette lighter and held it between the boards. "What are those noises?" she whispered.

"Draining, I guess," Stu said. "It's dark as pitch down there. I can't see anythin'."

"Stu?" Lidia said tremulously. "Let's nix on this. We can find another tree."

Didn't she realize it was too late to chicken out? It was just like Lidia not to realize they couldn't pull back now. Finding another tree would be a damn sight harder than it sounded, but that was hardly the point. This had become personal, a matter of defending his family's honor.

When he caught up with Leo and Arliss, Leo was gazing into the depths below him and asking his brother, "You sure you swum down there? You ain't psychin' me out?"

"I told you I did," Arliss insisted. Turning to Stu, he laid out the plan. "It's real simple. You and Leo are gonna swim over there and tag the far wall. First one back to the ladder claims all. Either side yellow-belly's, it's a forfeit. Y'all got that?"

Stu nodded. He got it. Simple? For Superman, maybe, or Tarzan. But for a mere kid like himself, it was a suicide swim in what sounded like the world's biggest toilet. Was Arliss telling the truth about swimming the pool? If Leo didn't believe his big brother, why should he?

Leo nervously chewed on his lip as he and Stu took off their shoes. They chose to see who would be first down the ladder. Stu lost. Gingerly, he started his descent into hell.

Whoever had named it "the devil's womb" had been right on target. The interior of the tank was dark as night, dank, and monstrously big. A few dim rays of light fell through the gaps in the platform, just enough for Stu to make out the enormous, bubbling pool twenty feet below him.

Foaming whirlpools, some of them as much as fifteen feet in diameter, churned through the water. It took no brains to figure out that any thing or person unlucky enough to get trapped in their vortexes would be instantly sucked to his death.

"Ah, Jesus," Leo moaned, a few inches above him.

Ten feet above water level, two long narrow ledges extended from either side of the ladder. The rest of the kids, who had followed them down the ladder, climbed out onto the two platforms as Stu and Leo reached point zero.

In the murky light, Stu could see the terror in Leo's eyes as he surveyed the pool that lay just beyond.

"There ain't no way across here," Leo quavered.

Stu had moved to a point beyond fear. He had flown through time and space to a jungle deep in South Vietnam. He was crawling on his belly alongside his father, stalking the Vietcong guerrillas who had ambushed him and Dodge.

"We'll find out, won't we?" he said calmly.

Leo stared at Stu as if he were crazy. Then he shook his head and clambered back up the ladder.

Arliss grabbed him as he reached the ledge. "What's goin' on?" he demanded.

"You ain't never been up here at all, have you? You swimmin' across here was a bunch of dick!" Leo cried.

"Ah, it ain't as bad as it looks!"

"It's worse than it looks! Anybody tries, they ain't comin' back!"

"Simmons ain't afraid of swimmin' it!" Arliss taunted him.

"That moron's crazier than you!" said Leo.

"You're goin' pussy on that kid?"

If Leo had the strength, he would have swung at his brother. As it was, he figured he was lucky to get out alive. "You swim it, why don't you?" he challenged him, continuing to climb his way back to solid ground.

"Fine! I will!" Arliss shouted after him. But as soon as Leo had vanished over the top of the tower, he turned to Willard. "You go down there," he ordered him.

Willard's answer came without a second's hesitation. "I ain't goin' down there."

"Willard, don't you knuckle on me! You want them to think we's chicken shit?" Arliss muttered.

Willard shrugged, as if to say, better chicken shit than dead, and Arliss went on down the line. "Ebb? Darla?"

They both shook their heads vigorously. He had no takers.

Stu was watching the negotiation from his

precarious perch down below. His teeth were chattering with tension, but he was nevertheless enjoying Arliss' predicament. "Did somebody call this off and forget to tell me?" he called up to them.

Arliss glared at his brothers and sisters, silently demanding a volunteer. They stood stiff as statues.

"Okay for all of you!" he declared. "But when I lay claim to that tree house, and I will, ain't none of you settin' foot-one inside!"

His threat didn't move them. Arliss swung off the ledge and came down the ladder to join Stu.

"Where's Leo?" Stu asked.

Arliss seemed not to hear the question. He stared at the menacing waters swirling just below his feet as if he were facing them for the very first time. It hit Stu then with absolute certainty that Arliss had never been down this far before. He had lied about having swum the pool. He looked scared to death, and Stu was about to call his bluff.

He said, "Ready? We'll cut right between those two swirls. . . ." He looked at Arliss but got no response. "On your mark, get set—"

"Hold on!" Arliss blurted out. "Look here. I'm gonna give you one chance to back out. You give me the word, we'll think up a different deal, for your sake."

Stu felt a mix of relief and disappointment. "You forfeitin'?" Again no response from Arliss, who looked paralyzed with fear. Stu decided to go for broke. "Lidia," he yelled. "Count us down!"

Lidia crossed her fingers and prayed for Arliss to chicken out. She began, "On your mark . . ."

"Son-of-a-bitch!" Arliss snapped. "You know there ain't no way."

"Get set . . ." Lidia's voice floated above them. Stu readied himself for the plunge.

"Go!"

Stu hit the water. Arliss didn't move.

The next second, a ten-foot piece of wood came crashing down from the platform. It hurtled into the pool like an oversized harpoon, creating tidal wave surges of water. Arliss struggled not to lose his grip. Stu grabbed for the ladder. He had just barely managed to haul himself up the rungs to safety when the board got swallowed up in the maelstrom.

He was shuddering so violently he had to rest a moment before he could follow Arliss up the ladder. One thought consoled him; Arliss had forfeited the dare. The ordeal was finished. The fort still belonged to him.

When he finally made it up to the platform, the Lipnickis were getting ready to descend the side of the tower. "Boy, I psyched you out!" yelled Arliss, trying to save face. "You thought we were really gonna swim it! What a cretin!"

Stu was too wiped out to remind him of the truth. "The lot's ours," he said.

"So have it! We never wanted your shitty old fort in the first place!"

"Hey! . . . The lock?" Stu called, holding out his hand.

"Give him the lock," Arliss told Willard.

Willard shook his head. "No."

"I said, give it!"

"No!" Willard said again.

Fed up with his passel of unmindful brothers and sisters, Arliss hauled off and smashed Willard across the nose. Hatred flashed in Willard's eyes as he grudgingly pulled out the lock and key and flung them at Stu.

The lock fell at Stu's feet. The key sailed past him and landed on a rotting plank on the far side of the platform.

"Go get it, why don't you? I dare you!" Willard jeered.

Arliss threw him a dirty look and started down the ladder. The rest of his family came after him. Only Billy stayed behind, watching Stu break off a sliver of wood to try and retrieve the key.

"Move it, Billy!" Ula screamed up at him.

He edged toward the ladder, wanting to see Stu succeed. But the key was too far, the risk of the plank cracking too great. Stu shrugged his shoulders in defeat. Billy sadly climbed over the side of the tower as Stu's friends closed in to console him.

Chet clapped Stu on the back to congratulate him for his bravery. "Hey! What say us guys camp out at the fort tonight? We'll bring junk to eat from my house. It'll be cool," he said.

Stu nodded. He hated to lose the key, but he felt good about what he had done. He had stood up to the Lipnickis and won an important battle. He knew his father would be proud of him today.

Lidia was cooking again. Even before Stu walked in the house, he was prepared for the worst by the cloud of thick black smoke pouring through the window. He thought, *Geez!* As if his day hadn't been dangerous enough! Now he had to eat supper in the middle of a fire-hazard zone. He came into the kitchen and pretended to gag at whatever it was she was torturing to death in the frying pan.

It had been raining heavily since early afternoon, and the roof was leaking badly. Lois had placed tin cans at strategic places all over the house to catch the water; Stu emptied the one on the table and sat down across from Stephen, who was watching the news.

"How's Lidia doing with supper?" Lois called from the bedroom.

"She's napalming the meat good," Stu assured her. "Me and the boys are goin' to sleep at the fort tonight, if that's okay."

"Me, too," Lidia announced.

Stu opened his mouth to say, no way, man. But his mother beat him to the punch. "That's fine if it stops rainin'," she agreed.

Stu ignored Lidia's gleeful cackle and stared at the TV set. Footage of the war, translated into black and white, flickered across the screen: President Nixon explaining why the United States had invaded Cambodia; a squadron of B-52's dropping bombs over Cambodia; student peace demonstrators at Kent State University getting shot by Ohio National Guardsmen. Walter Cronkite's voice provided the thread that bound the images together.

Stu listened closely, trying to understand what Cronkite was saying about the war in southeast Asia. He was about to ask his father why the students had been killed in Ohio when Lois walked by and bent to kiss him.

She turned to kiss Stephen and saw that he was almost in tears. Without saying a word, she switched to the next channel, where a couple of policemen were having a shoot-out with three masked men in a bank. She tried the next channel. A bare-chested karate master was hammering his opponent with his hands and feet. Disgusted by the relentless violence, she clicked off the set and put her arms around Stephen.

"I think I'm about done," said Lidia.

"It's definitely killed, whatever it was," Stu said.

Lois reached up to stroke her husband's cheek. She said, "Stephen? That's all a million miles from here. Besides, everything's going great now. Stopped rainin' just for mealtime. Come to the table."

Stephen kissed her fingers, dried his eyes with the edge of her apron, and smiled crookedly. He wondered, as he sat down, whether the war would ever end. The machine kept on going. The killing never stopped. He was a simple, uneducated man, not a politician or a general. But he had seen the war up close. For the life of him, he couldn't understand how all that spilled blood was going to do a damn bit of good in the world.

"So this evening's for celebratin'," he said, turning to Stu and trying to put a cheerful face on things. "Lidia told me that you settled your argument with the Lipnickis by usin' your wits, not your fists. I'm proud of you."

Stu grinned. Old blabbermouth Lidia had finally told something worth telling.

"Work's good at the mine," Stephen went on. "And Mom's—"

Lois shook her head, not yet ready to reveal her secret. "—and Mom's content," Stephen said, winking at his wife. "So, Stu?"

Stu bent his head. "Bless this food," he said. "Please!"

"Why's he always do the blessin' like that, Daddy?" Lidia asked suspiciously.

"It helps his digestion, sweetheart," he said, and tried to look enthusiastic as he dug into his plate of lumpy, burned chicken stew.

The rain had stopped, but the evening was overcast and cool when all six kids gathered after supper at the fort. True to his word, Chet brought candy bars and potato chips, which they washed down with soda pop and cigarettes. A co-ed poker game kept them amused until it got too dark to read the cards, even with their flashlights beamed on high.

Then Elvadine got the idea to turn off the flashlights and tell ghost stories. She went first, with a story about a headless horseman who rode the highways by the light of the full moon, searching for the man whose head could replace the one he lost. Next, Lidia told her favorite, about the man with the claw hand who preyed on innocent young couples parked in lovers' lanes.

As Lidia screamed out the punch line, the wind started blowing through the branches, rattling the windows. Marsh yawned loudly and said he was pretty near ready to go to sleep. Stu suspected that Marsh was more scared than tired, particularly when Marsh clutched at his BB gun and suggested that they leave one flashlight on, "just in case."

"In case of what?" Lidia wanted to know.

"Emergencies, dummy," Marsh retorted. "Like if someone has to pee or something in the middle of the night."

Stu supposed he was right. The moon and stars were totally hidden behind the clouds. It was so dark that he could barely make out his own fingers. The night surrounded them like a solid black wall, dense and impenetrable.

They snuggled into their blankets, tossed about until they got comfortable on the hard wood surface, and whispered amongst themselves until one by one, they finally fell asleep.

Stu was back in the water tower, dreaming about diving for lost medals, when he heard the headless horseman calling to him on the wind. He pulled himself out of the dream and sat up slowly. Fully awake, he heard the sound again.

"Woooo. . . ."

"Hey, what the hell's that?" he said, startling the other kids awake. Marsh grabbed his gun, ready for action.

"Woooo. . . ." The noise came again.

"It sounds like a ghost," Elvadine said, switching on her flashlight. Her eyes were round as saucers as she played the light over the darkened corners of the room.

"Aw, shit, man!" Marsh muttered. "What if we built this place on an Indian burial ground? My dad said Mississippi's loaded with pissed-off Chickasaws, their bones just layin' round waitin' to take revenge on the white man. One time, me and my old man went fishin' and—"

"Shut up, Marsh," said Stu.

"All right. But what do we do?"

Stu crept across the floor and unlatched a window. The other kids followed. A whiff of the sweetly scented night air brought him back to reality; there was no such thing as headless horsemen. Someone was playing games with them.

"Who's out there?" he called.

"Whooo, it's the ghost," came a voice that could only belong to Billy Lipnicki.

Chet giggled with relief. "Jeez, it's Billy!"

"Get outta town, you little narc! You spilled your guts about this place!" Marsh yelled.

"I didn't spill none of my guts," Billy sniveled.

"Then how'd they find out?" asked Chet.

"Well . . . I told them," Billy reluctantly admitted. "But they cut off my ear and they weren't gonna give it back."

"That's a trick they done with their thumb, you little dip! They didn't take your real ear," said Marsh.

After the pathetic haircut his brothers had given Billy, Chet couldn't blame the kid for falling for that dumb ear trick. "Why don't you go home, Billy, before they find out you're gone," he said, not unkindly.

He shut the window, but Billy wouldn't give up. "Wooo . . . ," he cried.

Marsh slammed open the window. "What?" he demanded.

"They locked me out. Said I had to sleep in the dog house."

"Good for them!" shouted Marsh.

Stu shone his flashlight down on Billy. His head was bent, and his shoulders were heaving with silent sobs. He felt sorry for the poor kid . . . no mother, a drunk for a father, no one to read him stories or wipe his nose or cuddle with him in bed when he felt sick the way Stu's mother always did.

"C'mon, you guys. He's just a little kid. He can't help it if he has assholes for brothers," he said.

Chet and Marsh opened their mouths to protest, but Stu cut them right off. "Come up, Billy," he called to the child. "You can sleep next to me."

Billy hurried up the ladder and into the fort. He curled up under Stu's blanket, and soon they were all sleeping soundly.

The rest of the night passed uneventfully. They woke up the next morning to a glorious summer dawn. The clouds had cleared, and sunlight was streaming through the windows.

Chet poked his head out from under his blanket and stared at the walls. "Jeez," he said sleepily. "Fallin' asleep in this pink room makes me dream I got my period."

Stu sat up and scratched his head. Billy was still curled up next to him, asleep or pretending to be. Everyone else was stretching and yawning and rubbing sleep out of their eyes.

Suddenly, they heard a thud at the door.

"Now what?" Lidia mumbled.

"Oh my God!" Chet poked an elbow in Marsh's ribs. "What if it's the Chickasaws?"

"Aw, eat my butt," said Marsh.

Stu stumbled over to the door and unlatched the lock. He hardly had a chance to step out of the way when all six Lipnickis dived into the room, screeching like a band of wild animals.

"Get outta here!" Stu yelled.

"You get out, dick!" Arliss yelled back.

Lidia, Elvadine, and Amber grabbed their blankets and jumped to their feet. Marsh glanced around for his BB gun, but Ebb got to it before he did.

"Hey, we won it far and square at the water tower!" said Marsh.

Arliss scratched his head and made a show of thinking long and hard. "I don't remember nothin' about no water tower! Thanks for house-sittin', shitheads!" he jeered.

Willard noticed what appeared to be a blanket creeping along the floor. He poked it with his foot. To his astonishment, his baby brother came tumbling out. "What the hell you doin' here, Billy?" he shouted. "You little traitor!"

"Go away!" Billy cried, as Willard kicked him in the leg.

"Knock it off!" yelled Stu, jumping to Billy's defense.

Still wrapped in their blankets, the girls watched

in horror as the rest of the Lipnickis got busy trashing the fort. While Ula and Darla were spray-painting their names all over the walls, the boys spread out across the room, smashing everything they could get their hands on. They caved in the stove and dented the chimney. Next, they ripped into the fruit crates and the lawn chairs. Then, Arliss and Leo went after the extra lumber they had left stacked against the wall.

"Get outta here!" Lidia screamed, chopping at them with her fists.

"It's ours now, butt-breath! Beat it!" Arliss screamed. He grabbed Lidia by the waist and pushed her out the door. The other two girls came flying after her. Stu, Chet, and Marsh fought hard, but they were an unequal match for the four Lipnicki boys, with Ula and Darla providing re-inforcements.

"You, too!" Arliss shouted at Billy, booting him out after the others.

The Lipnickis stood in the doorway, hooting with laughter at the sight of Amber sprawled on the ground, wearing only a baby doll nightie that barely covered her ample thighs. Lidia and Elva-dine tugged at their T-shirts as they hit the dirt. A second later, their clothes tumbled down on top of them, along with the shredded remains of the Uncle Sam poster and a shower of splintered crates.

"Look what I found!" Ebb cried, dancing and waving his arms from the lookout tower. "The war hero forgot his medals!"

"Hey, man! Those are his dad's! Give 'em here!" Chet shouted.

Ebb pinned them on his shirt and puffed out his chest. "They're mine now!" he exulted.

"Give 'em back, you son-of-a-bitch!" Stu roared, his resolve not to fight utterly forgotten.

"Come and get 'em!" Ebb taunted him, strutting back and forth across the roof.

Livid with rage, Stu and Lidia shinned up the tree to rescue the medals. Their progress was slowed by a hail of fruit—the oranges and apples they had brought for breakfast—showered down on their heads by Ula, Darla, and Leo. They kept on climbing, crawling from branch to branch until finally they reached the base of the fort.

Ula stood in the door. Grinning like a Halloween jack-o'-lantern, she raised her sneakered foot and brought it down with all her weight onto their hands.

"Ow!" Lidia howled. Stu groaned. They lost their grip and hit the ground in unison with a resounding thwack.

Stu leaped up and shook his fist at his enemies, who were cavorting on the roof of his fort. "You *swore* to us it was *ours*!" he bellowed.

"Why, that's an out-and-out lie," Leo said, dripping sarcasm. "Our daddy don't allow us to swear."

His brothers and sisters almost hurt themselves, they were laughing so hard.

For the first time in his life, Stu understood the urge to murder. His hatred of the Lipnickis was so intense that he could hardly breathe. Tears came to his eyes as he gasped for air.

"Come on." Chet took his arm. "We'll get everything back later."

"They're ruinin' everything," Lidia wept.

"They're not gonna keep my dad's medals!" Stu raged, shaking off Chet.

"We'll get them back and we'll fix the fort," Chet said, leading them away from the tree. "C'mon. We gotta get a plan."

CHAPTER ELEVEN

THE SIX children, trailed by Billy and his dog, straggled home through the woods, cursing the Lipnickis. Somebody had to teach those guys a lesson, Marsh kept saying. They all agreed with him. But first, the Lipnickis had to be evicted from the fort.

Lidia suggested that they get a court order from the sheriff to have the place condemned. "But then we won't be allowed to use it either," Stu pointed out.

Lidia said, oh, right. She hadn't thought of that.

"We could smoke them out by shooting tear gas down the chimney. I saw the cops do it on TV," Marsh said.

Stu and Chet liked that idea a lot, until Elvadine asked, wouldn't it take forever to air out the fort so that their eyes wouldn't be hurting from the gas?

Marsh still thought it was worth a try, but the rest of them voted him down. Besides, where would they get the tear gas from? It wasn't exactly the sort of thing people had lying around in the garage or that you could buy in the local hardware store.

The birds were chirping overhead, as if scolding them for not enjoying the blessing of a cloudless blue sky on this perfect July morning. Stu watched them swoop among the branches, flitting gaily from tree to tree. He almost couldn't bear to hear their song, which seemed to mock his wretchedly bleak mood. He had never felt so utterly betrayed—by the Lipnickis, whom he had stupidly trusted, and far worse, by his father.

His father believed that love kept people safe and happy. Well, Stu had tried, if not to love his enemies, at least to play fair and square with them. A lot of good it had done him. He was anything but happy this morning, and none of them would be safe until they got tough with those damned bullies. The hell with love. The Bible said, an eye for an eye, a tooth for tooth; a show of strength was the only language the Lipnickis would understand.

But what to do? He wished they *could* get hold of some tear gas. The thought of the Lipnickis flying out of the fort, crying and choking on the gas, made him feel almost cheerful. He broke a twig off a bush and threw it in the air, watching to see where it would land. The twig twirled through space, then floated on the breeze, an arrow in flight; then, as if by magic, it pointed him straight to the solution.

The other kids voted unanimously in favor of his plan. They hurried home to collect the necessary equipment: a pair of hedge clippers that Marsh's mother used to trim her garden; a large plastic trash bag; a couple of newspapers; a book of matches. Then they reassembled at the turnoff in the woods to undertake the offensive they had code-named "Operation Piñata."

Because it was his idea, and because the Lipnickis had stolen his dad's medals, Stu insisted he had to be the one to undertake the most dangerous part of the mission. No one gave him an argument on that score. A hornet's nest was nothing to fool with.

The nest dangled from a branch that was a couple of arms' lengths above their heads. Stu studied it as he stuck the clippers under his belt in the small of his back and rolled the newspaper sheets into the shape of a funnel. The matches went in his pocket. He was ready to move.

Holding the funnel in one hand, he climbed up the tree and shimmied out onto the branch that held the nest. Chet and Marsh stood just below, holding the trash bag open and ready. The girls, along with Billy and his dog, stood some feet away.

Stu took out the matches, and on the third try succeeded in lighting the newspaper. The funnel was instantly transformed into a flaming torch, which he carefully positioned just below the nest.

"Don't light them on fire," Marsh warned, anxiously monitoring the cloud of hornets swarming around the nest. "They get mean when you light them on fire."

"I'm just druggin' them," said Stu, who had already explained his strategy, which he had read about in one of his library books.

"Looks like it's workin'. They're all goin' inside," Elvadine said.

"Won't last for long," Stu said. "Okay, I'm cuttin' it. Get ready."

"Oh, man." Marsh moaned, holding tight to the garbage bag.

Stu threw down the torch, and the girls ran to stamp out the flames. Stretching himself out the length of the branch, he grabbed the top of the nest, clenched it between the blades of the clippers, and yanked hard to loosen it.

Just as he had hoped, the nest dropped neatly into the bag, which Chet and Marsh quickly tied shut with a strong knot.

"Billy, you better go home. Your brothers see you with us after what we're gonna do, they'll kill you," Stu said, sliding back down the tree.

Billy frowned. He wanted to stay with his new friends, who were much nicer to him than his family. "Why can't we share the fort?" he whined, wishing they could all play together there.

"Your brothers didn't live up to their word, now did they?" Stu asked.

Billy shook his head. With his very own ears, he had heard Arliss say they didn't even want the shitty old fort.

"They took my dad's medals. Do you think they'll share anything with us?"

Biting his lip to keep from crying, Billy slunk away, and Stu joined his friends on the shortcut to the fort. While the rest of the gang waited at the edge of the woods, he sneaked up the ladder and crept across the roof to the stovepipe.

He could hear the hornets buzzing angrily inside the bag even before he gave it a good shake that really stirred them up. He untied the knot and swiftly dumped the hive through the hole in the pipe. Then he leapt off the roof and raced back to the shelter of the woods.

It felt like the silence before a storm as they waited tensely for the Lipnickis' reaction.

"Maybe they left," whispered Chet. "Y'all think they left?"

Stu peered through the branches. At that precise moment, they heard blood-curdling screams. The door flew open. The six Lipnickis leaped out of the fort and threw themselves down the ladder.

Stu and his friends stepped out of the woods as the Lipnickis fled across the open field.

"This is total war, man! Your ass is grass!" Arliss screamed, holding aloft Stephen's medals for Stu to see them.

"How long 'til you figure they're back?" asked Chet.

"Maybe they won't be back. Maybe we taught them a lesson," Marsh said optimistically.

"They'll be back," Chet predicted. "Don't you think, Stu?"

Stu nodded grimly. "Of course they'll be back! How do you think I'm gonna get my medals?"

"I guess you know they gonna murder us as soon as they figure out how," said Elvadine.

"Chet, light the torch and clear out the fort," Stu said, staring after the Lipnickis. "We'll be ready for them."

Chet and Marsh rolled up another cone of

newspaper and cautiously climbed the ladder to smoke out the hornets.

Lidia sidled over to her brother and pulled him aside. All this talk about the Lipnickis coming back was making her nervous. Maybe they should just leave well enough alone, now that they had their fort back. Let the Lipnickis keep the damn medals. Their father would probably never know they were missing.

"What about Dad? He finds out we're fightin', he might go nuts again," she hissed in Stu's ear.

"Dad's way of thinkin' ain't gonna help us, Lidia. He'd just as soon we let them take everything, like the city done with our house."

He fought back tears as he stared after the retreating Lipnickis. "I love him, but he'd give up anything in order not to have to fight, even his medals which he fought to get. I'm doin' this for him as much as for us."

Stu's forces were officially at war with the Lipnickis. They won their first skirmish, Operation Piñata. The important battle was yet to be fought. First, they had to properly arm themselves. The troops fanned out across town to gather supplies.

Stu pulled out his father's footlocker again and searched through it for a talisman, some kind of good luck charm. Tucked away at the bottom of the trunk was a small brown envelope that contained two sets of dog tags. He took them out and read the names. One had been worn by his father. The other had been worn by Dodge. Now, he would wear them both when he fought the Lip-nickis.

In his big brother's closet, Marsh found a gold mine—twenty or so books on cheap and simple ways to make explosive devices. He checked the garage and hit pay dirt again. "Dig this, man!" he announced, arriving at the fort with an arm-load of books. "I checked my garage and found a whole bag of cherry bombs."

"That stuff's no problem. We can get M-80's, whatever we want, half-price at any stand now," Chet reminded them.

He was right, of course. Once the Fourth of July was past, most people had no more use for fire-works, which made this the perfect time to buy. They pooled their money and came up with a grand total of four and a half dollars. While everyone else stayed to dig trenches around the fort, Stu and Marsh hitchhiked to the highway entrance on the other side of town.

Sure enough, the sign on top of the red, white, and blue-decorated booth said, "All fireworks, half-price." The fellow at the stand had his feet up on the counter and looked bored. He glanced up from the magazine he was reading and said he was glad to see them. Business had been bad all week; he would give them an extra break on the price, just to get rid of the stuff.

He loaded them up with boxes of Roman candles, cherry bombs, and M-80's. "Always happy to see a satisfied customer," he said, pocketing their money. He went back to reading his magazine; they went back to stocking their arsenal.

Elvadine's aunt had an orchard of plum and peach trees behind her house. Whatever they could pick was theirs, she told the girls. The girls worked hard one entire afternoon, loading their wagons with the hard, unripened fruit.

Chet spent hours flat on his back, beneath his father's car, stuffing balloons with dirty oil from the crankcase. The next day, he and the other boys sneaked onto a construction site after quitting time. Holding their noses to keep from vomiting, they dipped bucket after bucket into the trough behind the outhouse, filling a ten-gallon double-strength bag with human waste.

The girls had mixed their own witches' brew in a barrel, a nauseating combination of motor oil and sour milk, to which the boys added the contents of the ten-gallon bag. The result looked vile, and the stench made them gag.

Then Marsh came up with the brilliant idea to test the recipe in the field. They carried a sackful of the stuff to his garage and pulled out the bag of cherry bombs. He lit one and tossed it inside the sack. They took cover and waited.

The bag exploded with a deafening blast. Sticky globs of shit and curdled milk sprayed all over Marsh's father's car. It smelled hideous. It would be hell to clean up. The recipe was judged a success.

The circumference of the fort was banked by trenches, which the boys had covered over with tarps. Now they were spreading leaves across the tarps as camouflage.

"Where are they?" Chet fretted, as he rigged trip wires between the bushes.

"They're so chicken-shit, they got a brown stripe running up and down their yellow backs," said Marsh, deepening one of the trenches.

"Marsh, if you'd dig with your mouth, instead of saying stupid things all day, we'd be finished by now," Stu said.

The tension was mounting. The ambush had been set. The weapons were all in place. The decoys had been deployed. They were ready for combat.

The decoys—Lidia and Elvadine—were treading on enemy territory, circling the quarry.

"Well, now you know what the worm feels like," said Elvadine, nervously checking her back.

"Huh?" said Lidia, who was nervous, too, but trying hard not to show it.

"We're danglin' on a hook for the Lipnickis to bite at."

Lidia caught a glimpse of movement behind a rock just ahead of them. "Don't look now, but I see some hungry Lipnickis to your left," she whispered.

"Why couldn't one of the boys be the bait?" Elvadine whimpered. "I think I'm gonna go wee-wee in my pants."

"I told you not to look!" said Lidia. "Clench your butt and get ready to run."

Too scared to talk, they continued as planned, walking across the exterior wall of the quarry. In the distance, they could see a figure waiting on the overpass that crossed their escape route. They moved closer and saw that it was Arliss; he was holding a long, thick metal chain.

Then he spotted them. He held up the chain and whirled it in a circle above his head, like a lasso. It was the signal his gang had been waiting for; at least two dozen kids, including Lester Lucket, came charging down the hill, jumping out from behind bushes and rocks, armed with chains and rocks.

"I knew this would happen," Elvadine cried.

They tore across the swampy wash, dodging the rocks that flew at them from all directions. The Lipnickis and their crew tore after them, moving closer and forming a wedge that would cut off any chance of escape.

Finally, as planned, they reached the water pipe that had been built into the overpass to provide drainage from the quarry. They scurried through the wide-mouthed opening and sprinted through the darkness. Lidia didn't dare turn around, but she could hear their pursuers' footsteps pounding behind them.

"Run!" she shouted to Elvadine, who was falling behind.

"I'm runnin'!" Elvadine yelled.

"Well, run faster!" she urged.

They saw the light that meant they were close to the other end of the pipe. Then they were outside, and the fort was in sight.

Stu was stationed in a tree, scanning the field through his father's binoculars. He spotted Lidia first and called to Marsh, "Here she comes."

"They followin' them?" asked Marsh, who was sitting in a tree a few feet closer to the fort.

"Hell, they got the whole town behind them!" said Stu.

"No way!" Marsh exclaimed. Then he spoke into his walkie-talkie. "They're comin' in, guys. More than we expected!"

Amber and Chet, who was dressed in his full football uniform, were crouched in a fox hole at the foot of the fort. Next to the them was a wooden cola-bottle case, filled with bottle rockets aimed and ready to fire. A board lay across the hole, and they raised it now to scout the enemy's approach.

Lidia and Elvadine darted up the ladder and disappeared inside the fort. Arliss' gang barreled after them.

"Now!" screamed Stu.

Marsh had armed himself with a supply of the lethal cherry bomb-glop combination. At Stu's command, he lit a sack and hurled it at the invading force. It detonated just as they got to the ladder, showering the bunch of them with gluey hunks of rancid debris.

Before they had a chance to figure out what had hit them, a round of bottle rockets blasted through the air.

"Kill 'em!" Arliss roared.

Marsh set off another round of oil bombs. Lidia and Elvadine were using slingshots to pelt their foe with the fruit and rocks they had stocked in the fort. Leo hit the ground, felled by a well-aimed rock in his groin. Other kids toppled into the camouflaged trenches or tumbled over the trip wires. The Lipnicki gang tried to repel their attackers; but they were at a disadvantage on the lower ground, and their weapons were limited to the handful of rocks they had brought with them.

Lidia was aiming a plum at Arliss when she thought she saw a garbage can stumbling across the battlefield. She took a second look and saw a pair of dirty overalls and bare feet sticking out from the bottom of the can. She figured it could only be Billy, turning up as usual where he shouldn't be. The sides of the garbage can were getting bludgeoned by all the stray ammo. A direct hit from a flying rock knocked the can onto its side and sent Billy spinning toward one of the trenches.

His brothers were all close by, but none of them saw him. Arliss had set his sights on getting Stu. Dodging the barrage of flying objects, he scaled the tree where Stu was positioned, climbed out onto a nearby branch, and grabbed Stu's arm. The two boys grappled in midair, each struggling to throw the other off balance, until both plunged to the ground. They rolled in the dirt, clawing and pounding at each other's heads and faces, intent on doing serious damage.

Suddenly, Lidia whipped around the corner and torpedoed Arliss with a well-aimed missile from her slingshot. He threw up his hands to protect himself. Stu squirmed out of his grasp and got away.

"Arliss!" Billy cried, running over to comfort his brother.

"Aw, Billy, get lost! You're useless! Just beat it

before you get hurt!" Arliss yelled, and ran to look for Willard and Leo.

He found them, bruised and drenched in muck, at the back of the fort, filling their tube socks with rocks.

"What are y'all hidin' out here for?" he demanded.

Leo held up a sock. "We're tryin' to make weapons. They're creamin' us!" he said.

"Willard! C'mon! Now!" Arliss barked.

Willard dragged himself to his feet and followed his commander back into the fray.

Lidia had gotten distracted searching for Billy. She didn't see Lester sneaking up behind her until he grabbed her shoulder and bent one of her arms behind her back.

"All them times you knocked out my teeth! I'm gonna show you now!" he threatened, shoving his chain under her nose.

Just in time, Elvadine came to her rescue. She took careful aim with her wrist-rocket and whopped him in the mouth.

"That was my last front tooth! You knocked out my last front tooth!" he screamed and ran off to tell his mother.

With Arliss temporarily out of the picture, Stu had gone in search of Ebb. He found him trying to sneak up on Marsh, who was still firing oil bombs from his tree.

"Give me my dad's medals," he said, stepping between Ebb and the tree.

"Come and get 'em," Ebb sneered.

He grabbed a shovel and swung it at Stu. Stu

dodged the blow. Ebb swung again. Stu ducked and snatched up a rock. He flung it at Ebb and hit him in the chest.

"You turd!" Ebb cried.

"Give them back to me," Stu yelled. "Or I swear to God—"

"You'll do what? Cry? Like the last time? Wah, wah . . . 'He took my dad's medals!'" Ebb leered at Stu and swatted him with the shovel. Stu managed to knock him to the ground. They wrestled a moment until Ebb pulled free and jumped to his feet.

He dangled the medals just out of Stu's grasp and laughed. "You're never gonna get 'em!" he said.

Then he dropped them into his mouth, seemingly prepared to swallow them. Stu charged and smashed him in the stomach. The medals popped out of Ebb's mouth and onto the ground. The boys dived after them.

"Give them to me!" Stu yelled.

Ebb landed a sharp kick in his chest that knocked the wind out of him. He struggled for air, caught his breath, and grabbed Ebb's foot, bringing him down. He pounced on top of him and punched him with all the strength he could summon, until Ebb gave up and stopped struggling.

Spent and exhausted, Stu picked up the medals. He turned to walk away when Ebb grabbed hold of his leg. At the touch of Ebb's hand on his flesh, he felt something snap inside himself. He had tried to make peace with Ebb and his brothers. He had matched his courage against theirs and won. Now he beat them again with his muscle, and thus betrayed the promise he had made to his father. *But Ebb still wouldn't let go of him.* He hated Ebb, hated all of the Lipnickis for their bullying ways and their cruelty and for making him into the fighter he didn't want to be.

His body quivered with unspent rage as he bent to pick up a rock and held it above Ebb's head. He was breathing too hard and too fast as he got ready to flatten Ebb's skull.

And then, as if he had come out of nowhere, Billy stood staring up at him. Stu carefully set the rock back down on the ground. The war had gone far enough.

It didn't take much longer for the Lipnickis to realize they had been defeated. When Chet screamed, "Victory or death!" they seemed to take him seriously and beat a hasty retreat. This time, there were no departing threats about a rematch. Nevertheless, Stu wasn't convinced he had seen the last of them.

Still, he had plenty to celebrate. He had reclaimed his father's medals. He and his friends had recovered their fort. They had hurt the Lipnickis and beaten them at their own game.

Marsh made up a victory chant, and the others danced as he sang:

> "We killed them!
> We destroyed them!
> We took no prisoners!
> Yaaaay!!"

CHAPTER TWELVE

AFTER DODGE, Stephen hadn't seen much point in getting friendly with the other men in his platoon. He kept to himself, figuring that he couldn't risk watching yet another buddy die under fire when he should have been there to save him. He was branded a loner, a label that hadn't much bothered him. He was never one to feel comfortable in a crowd or to go along with whatever the gang was up to.

In high school, he palled around with a couple of his football teammates. But they lost touch after he joined the army, and he hadn't taken the trouble to look them up since he had been back in town. He wasn't deliberately avoiding them, but by nature he was shy, and he had taken too many blows in the last few years to easily pick up the friendships where they had left off.

Stephen didn't easily put his trust in other people, much less himself. Then he had met up with Little Moe, who was a hard guy not to like. Little Moe was solid and dependable, with a jokey style that masked a keen, intuitive intelligence. It slowly dawned on Stephen that they had gotten to be friends.

They dug potatoes together under the broiling sun, and they generally drew the same shift and work detail at the mine. They enjoyed each other's humor and company. They made a good team, working hard and efficiently to get the job done.

On the same afternoon that their kin were waging war on the Lipnickis, the supervisor had assigned them to shore up a narrow caveway that connected two of the main shafts. They had talked during their coffee break about buying some beer after work and watching the baseball game on TV. Now, Stephen could almost taste the beer on his tongue as he replaced the rotted boards in the ceiling of the caveway.

He heard the rumble of thunder above his head and thought it strange for a storm to be coming up on a day that had been so clear three hours earlier when he had started his shift. He picked up his hammer, and a second rumble reverberated through the shaft. It hit him then that he was too far underground to be hearing thunder.

"Moe!" he yelled, as a third, much louder blast exploded in his ears.

A torrent of water cascaded through the ceiling and flung him onto the ground. He must have momentarily lost consciousness from the impact, because when he came to, he was floundering in water up to his chest. The shaft to his left, where earlier he and Little Moe had sat to drink their coffee, was now completely flooded. The narrow airway that led to the shaft on his right was also quickly filling up with water.

He tried swimming toward the airway, but the

water was gushing down with such velocity that he felt as if he were fighting upstream through rapids. He took a deep breath and dived underwater, stroking as hard as possible. When he came up for air, he was inside the larger of the two shafts.

"Moe!" he shouted, shining his helmet lantern into the darkness. His voice echoed off the marble walls. No answering call echoed back at him. He tried again. "Little Moe!" Still no answer.

Without stopping to think, he dived under again and swam back into the airway. He broke the surface and yelled, "Moe!"

This time he got a response. "Over here!" Little Moe said weakly.

Stephen swam toward Little Moe's voice. He found him pinned against the wall of the cavern, wedged between two large marble boulders. The water was still rising, but more slowly now. Little Moe was submerged up to his waist, but the rest of him was dry.

"I can't move," he said.

"Let me see." Stephen maneuvered himself into the corner and threw his weight against the boulder closest to him. The rock didn't budge even an inch. He looked around and saw one of the steel poles they had brought down to reinforce the ceiling. He grabbed the pole and warned Little Moe, "This isn't gonna feel good."

He jammed the pole underneath the boulder and levered with all the force he could muster.

"Ow! It ain't no use!" Little Moe cried. "Get out of here while you can."

"You know I can't do that. You still owe me twenty-five dollars," Stephen said, resting on the pole as he panted to catch his breath. "Hold on."

He leaned again on the pole and strained to create some give. The boulder slowly shifted a scant couple of inches, enough for Moe to pull free. He reached for Stephen's hand at the same moment that a shower of rocks collapsed on top of them and knocked out Stephen's lantern.

"Stephen?" said Little Moe. He groped for him in the dark. "Stephen?"

The only sound he heard was the water lapping against the sides of the cave.

Their hard-fought victory had made Lidia and Elvadine desperate for ice cream. They walked into town, hoping that Lidia's mother would treat them to cones at the Dixie Queen. They checked each other for wounds and decided they looked presentable. A couple of scratches, a bruise or two, a torn pocket. . . . Not bad, considering what they had just been through. Lois would never know, unless Lidia decided to tell her, that they had survived the Battle of Conner's Ridge.

Elvadine plopped down on the bench outside the Dixie Queen. "I need a smoke," she said.

"Don't let my mom see you," Lidia warned and went inside to negotiate with her mother for the cones.

The street was mostly empty except for the truck coming up the block. Elvadine happily puffed at her cigarette, swinging her feet as she sang the nonsense rhyme that was running through her head:

"Lester Lucket got me mad, So Lester Lucket made me bad.

Now Lester Lucket's really sad, 'Cause he got no front teeth to show his dad."

She giggled to herself, thinking she needed to make up more verses to sing to Lidia. Good old Lester. Boy, hadn't he looked stunned when she bopped him in the mouth!

"There's the colored girl," she suddenly heard someone scream.

She looked up. Ula was hanging out of the truck she had noticed a minute ago, which was now parked in front of the Dixie Queen. Darla and Willard were with her. The driver got out, and she saw that it was their father.

"Stay in the truck," she heard him say to the three children.

Mr. Lipnicki looked every bit as bloodthirsty as she had imagined him. She got up to run into the Dixie Queen, but it was too late. He had already stomped up the stairs and cornered her.

"You been stealin' from my property, girl. You kicked my boy's nuts. Where you come off thinkin' you can pull off a stunt like that, huh?" he demanded.

"Well," she said, her voice cracking from fear. She told herself to be brave. Mr. Lipnicki was nothing but a bully, just like his gutless kids. She stared into his red-rimmed eyes and said, "He started it."

He grabbed her sleeve and snarled, "Don't you

back talk to me! I got a mind to swat you good right now, so you never get no notion to attack one of my kin again. You hear me?"

"I ain't done nothin' wrong," she said, trying to pull away. "You watch your hands or I'll get my brother on you!"

"Don't threaten me, you fresh thing!" he said, yanking her arm as if she were nothing but a rag doll.

Lois and Lidia came running out of the Dixie Queen. "You let go of her," cried Lidia.

Lois pulled Lidia behind her. She glared at Lipnicki and said, "You take your hands off this child right this second before I have you hauled off to jail quicker than you can say holy roller."

Drawn by the commotion, a crowd had gathered on the pavement. Lipnicki was not a well-liked man, and most of the spectators were eager to see him bested.

"Best you get away before you get in trouble, too," he muttered.

Lois had known John Lipnicki since they were children. He hadn't scared her then, and he certainly didn't scare her now. "C'mon, hit me if you're such a tough guy," she invited him. "Hit me! At least I'm your age."

The crowd was growing and becoming more vociferous in its support of Lois. Sensing their hostility, Lipnicki growled, "I ain't gonna hit you nor this stupid nigger girl. But I tell you this, if either of these children come near my property again or touch my kin, they won't be wanderin' home again. You get my gist?"

As if to underscore his point, he spat at Elvadine, but the wad of saliva fell short of its mark. He smirked at Lois, who had to forcibly restrain Lidia from punching him, and turned to the onlookers. "Fire's out. You can all go back to your merry ways," he said. Then he got into his truck and drove off.

"Thank you, Miss Simmons," said Elvadine. She rubbed at the red, throbbing mark on her skin where Lipnicki had gripped her arm.

"I'm sorry you had to listen to that filth," Lois said.

"Mom, you showed him!" Lidia said. "Stood right up to his stupid face."

Lois sighed. She took no satisfaction from confronting such a pathetic soul as John Lipnicki. "Let's just forget about him. He's the kind give Southerners a bad name."

She was about to remind the girls about their ice creams when one of her coworkers slammed open the Dixie Queen door and spoke the words that were every miner's wife's nightmare.

"There's been an explosion at the mine, and they can't find Stephen or Little Moe."

A group of anxious relatives stood at the face of the mine, waiting for news of their loved ones. Some of the women were crying. Many were holding hands and praying as the rescue workers continued evacuating men from the shaft on stretchers.

With the children at her side, Lois rushed over to the harried foreman and said, "I'm Lois Simmons. My husband is Stephen Simmons. Is he okay?"

The foreman consulted his list. "He's down there, but he's been located. They should have him and Little Moe out any moment now."

"Are they okay?" Lois pressed him for details.

"We haven't had a fatality in this mine for over twenty years," he said, trying to encourage her. "Just keep your fingers crossed."

"He's too tough to be killed like this. They couldn't even kill him in a war," Stu said confidently.

Elvadine watched a paramedic apply a tourniquet to a miner's profusely bleeding wound. She thought about Little Moe, and the tears she had been suppressing flowed down her cheeks. Then Lidia was crying, too.

"I told you he wouldn't die now," Stu yelled.

Lois put her arm around her son's shoulder. She understood his anger and wished she could tell him, it's okay, don't worry. I know he won't die. But they had almost lost Stephen once before. She was too frightened of losing him now to tempt fate by making any false promises.

After what seemed like hours, Little Moe was brought out of the shaft in a mine car. His leg was wrapped in a splint, but he was conscious and managed a smile for Elvadine.

"You okay?" she asked, starting to cry again.

He nodded and squeezed her hand weakly. "Yes, I am."

"Where's my dad?" said Stu.

"They're bringin' him out. He saved my life," Little Moe said, as he was being loaded into the ambulance.

Stephen came out in the next car after Little Moe's. He lay on the stretcher, so pale and helpless that he seemed more dead than alive to Lois. He managed to twist his lips into a faint imitation of a smile that alarmed Lois more than it consoled her.

"Dad!" said Lidia. His shirt had been ripped away, and she stared at his chest, which was raw and bloody.

"Dad! Are you okay?" Stu said.

Stephen saw the terror in his family's faces and found the strength to whisper through his pain, "Of course I am."

"Sorry, son." An ambulance attendant stepped in front of Stu and signaled to his colleague. "We got to get him to the hospital in a hurry." The two men lifted Stephen's stretcher into the ambulance.

"Dad?" Stu said.

Stephen flashed him a thumbs up sign, not to worry. Then the doors closed in Stu's face, and the ambulance sped off, its sirens blaring.

The hospital waiting room was a cold, uninviting area with battered furniture and overly bright lighting that seemed as if it had been specially installed to highlight the fear and tension on everyone's faces. The nurse at the reception area had no answers for anyone's questions. She helped Lois fill out Stephen's admittance forms, and tried to be sympathetic, but she couldn't say when the doctor would be out to speak to them.

Lois kept telling herself it was a good sign that the doctor was taking so long with Stephen. It meant there were things that could be done to make him get better. He was young and strong, in perfect health. Stu was right. Stephen was too tough to die. And too stubborn.

The twins and Elvadine sat on the couch like three scared little mice, hardly daring to move. She had never seen them stay so quiet for so long. Stu had hardly said a word since they had gotten to the hospital.

He seemed to have gone to some place deep inside himself, as if he were communing with whatever spiritual power he trusted to heal his father. Lois understood. He *needed* his father. Both the children did, but Stu particularly had missed Stephen while he had been in Vietnam. Lidia was more resilient and feisty. Stu took after his daddy; he was thoughtful and shy, a leader in spite of himself.

There were other women in the room whose husbands had also been injured in the explosion. One of them, whose husband's arms had both been broken, wept silently into her handkerchief, refusing any offers of comfort from the older woman who sat next to her.

The doctor had already been out to speak to them. He had tried to joke with her, saying her husband would be fine, though he wouldn't be washing many dishes for a while. Lois wanted to tell her to stop crying. Broken arms could be mended.

Of course, the poor man would most likely be out of work for months. The union disability check was a fraction of what he could earn in the mine. No wonder his wife was worried.

"Mrs. Simmons?" The doctor finally came out of the operating room and motioned her over, out of earshot of the children.

"Is he gonna be all right?" she asked.

The doctor said, "His chest was crushed by the rock, and his heart badly bruised." He had no jokes for her about the dishes.

"I want to see him," she said.

The doctor nodded. "He's conscious now."

She was ready for the wires and tubes that connected him to all the machinery in the room. But she was shocked by his ashen complexion. It was as if all the blood had been drained from his face. Much of his chest was heavily bandaged, and where the bandages stopped, she could see a bright purple bruise.

"You had to save his life, didn't you?" she said, taking his hand.

"How else were we gonna get back the twenty-five dollars?" he rasped, trying to smile.

"God, I hate your sense of humor," she said, and though she had promised herself she wouldn't, she began to cry.

He tugged at her hand, pulling her closer. She laid her head on his shoulder. His breathing sounded labored in her ear.

"Everything's gonna work out," he whispered, his voice breaking.

"It better," she told him, and gave herself this time to be with him.

Lidia wished her mother would hurry on back to the waiting room. She was tired of waiting, and she wanted to know how her father was doing. Stu had said he wouldn't die, and she believed him. Still, she would have liked to see him herself, so she could stop being scared. Maybe then the sick feeling in her stomach that she'd had all afternoon would go away.

The waiting room had filled up with more people. Lidia noticed a couple of them staring at Elvadine, giving her funny looks. Elvadine must have noticed them, too, because she nudged Lidia and whispered, "I'll wait for your daddy outside."

Was Elvadine going to let some dumb white folks chase her out of the hospital? Lidia couldn't let her do that. "No. You can wait with us."

"I want to go outside," Elvadine said.

"Elvadine. . . ."

She shook off Lidia's hand. She needed to breathe some fresh air that wasn't tainted by such ignorant, trashy people. Lidia was her best friend for life, but some things were always going to be beyond her experience or comprehension.

She walked outside and sat on the lawn. The sun was getting lower, but the dew hadn't fallen yet and the grass felt soft and warm. She leaned against the building and began to sing her favorite hymn, "Amazing Grace."

Her voice floated through the open window in Stephen's room. "Elvadine?" he whispered.

Lois nodded. She hardly trusted herself to speak. She knew, from watching her mother die, that Stephen was dying. She didn't know how she could bear for that to happen. He had needed to be a hero, to prove to himself what she and everyone else already knew about him—that he wasn't a coward. It made no sense at all, and yet that didn't seem to matter.

She thought she understood about death, about its randomness and finality. But this was her husband. She loved him too damn long to say goodbye.

"I'm gonna bring the kids in," she said.

"Help me," he said. "I don't want to get all weepy in front of them."

She nodded, praying she wouldn't get all weepy herself, and went to fetch them. She didn't know what to say to prepare them, so she said nothing as she brought them into the room.

They rushed to his bedside.

"Are you okay, daddy?" Lidia asked.

"I'm fine, firecracker," he said with a feeble smile.

"You don't look fine," Lidia said, hating Stu for being so wrong this one time. "You look real bad."

"That's because I need you to cook me breakfast."

Tears spilled out of her eyes. Lois took her hand to lead her outside. "I love you, Dad," she said from the doorway.

"I love you, too, baby," he said and waved

goodbye. The effort took its toll. He moaned as a stabbing pain knifed through his chest. "Stuart?"

"Yeah?" said Stu, suddenly aware of the bruises he had sustained earlier.

"I'm so proud of you," he said, speaking so softly that Stu had to bend to hear him. "You're my prize. You know that?"

"Yes, sir. And you're my prize," said Stu.

He fingered the medals in his pocket and thought of all the things he wanted to tell his father: to keep on fighting to get well and not give up; and about today's battle, how he and his friends had once and for all beaten the Lipnickis and won back their fort.

"I know we had dark days," Stephen said. "But the day you and your sister were born was the day I knew God shined his light on me. No matter what happens, remember how much light you brought into my life." He touched a finger to Stu's cheek. "Now I want you to watch out for your mom and your sister. You promise me that?"

Stu nodded. He had already been watching out for them for such a long time that he wouldn't know how not to. "But you are comin' home?" he asked nervously.

"Just while I'm gone," Stephen said.

"Yes, sir. . . . Daddy?"

"Yeah?"

Stu needed to hear it again. "You are comin' home, aren't you?"

"For good," Stephen whispered, and then he fell asleep.

Stu lay down beside him and held his hand. Then Lois and Lidia came in, and while Elvadine sang outside the window, they stood guard and watched him sleep.

After a time, the nurse tiptoed into the room and asked them to leave. The doctor stopped to talk to Lois while Stu and Lidia paced the hall.

Stu wanted to ask the doctor whether they could stay the night in his father's room. He worried that his father might wake up and need something and no one would be there to get it for him.

Something else gave him cause for worry. "You think he knew we were fightin' again?" he asked Lidia.

"No," she said, in a tone that said, what do *you* think?

He told her what he felt in his heart. "I do."

CHAPTER THIRTEEN

LOIS CAME into the waiting room, where Stu and
Lidia had dozed off on the couch. She shook Stu
awake and spoke the hardest words he would ever
have to hear. "Your daddy died, Stu," she said
gently.

"No!" he said, so loudly that Lidia woke up.
"No!"

Lois repeated what the doctor had told her. "It
wasn't painful. He never even woke up, the doctor
says. His heart just quit pumpin'. The doctor says
the rock just crushed his heart and broke it."

"He's gonna be okay," Stu insisted, as Lidia
began to cry. "He can't die! He's on machines!"

Lois knew he was angry. She felt angry, too, but
there was no one—not even Stephen—to blame
for his death. "Son, they took him off the machines," she explained.

"Well, tell them to put him back on!" He stared
at her accusingly, as if he had just discovered she
was an accomplice to murder.

"Honey, he's gone," she said, wishing, for his
sake, that he could accept the awful reality. "They
can't now."

"Quit sayin' that! He's gonna be fine! Why'd

they take him off?" he cried. Slowly, the realization came to him. "Because it cost too much!"

Lidia gasped. She stared at Lois, wanting to know was that so? Lois wearily shook her head. "No."

But Stu was not so easily convinced. Money, or the lack of it, was a familiar nemesis. "Then why?" he challenged her.

"Because there was no hope. His heart was broken, and they couldn't fix it."

She put her arm around him, but he shrugged her off. He crossed his arms over his chest, a graphic "keep off" sign. "No! Everybody gave up on him!"

"Everybody" of course, included her and maybe Stu himself, as well? "Nothing could have kept your father from bein' with you, given he had a choice."

"Mama?" Lidia sobbed.

"What, honey?"

Lidia curled herself into Lois' lap. "You think he's stopped hurtin' now? You think he'll be okay?"

"He's in the Lord's hands now, and they're good hands," Lois said, grateful for her daughter's ability to make peace with her pain by finding the good.

Stu was a different story. "They gave up on him," he muttered.

She had known he would take it badly. She hadn't expected him to cast around for blame and fasten onto the hospital staff.

"Stu . . ."

"They didn't try hard enough."

"I bet he's lookin' down on us from heaven right now," Lidia said tearfully.

"I bet he is, too," Lois agreed, stroking Lidia's head. "He's in a place now where he'll be able to look out for us the rest of our lives."

"Well, I sure as hell hope he does a better job than when he was alive!" Stu burst out.

"Don't say that, Stu! You don't know . . . he could have been an angel. He could have died in that war, and maybe God sent him back here for one last visit," Lidia said. "Right, Mamma?"

"For what?" Stu shouted. "To get our hopes up? To promise us he'd stay forever, and we're gonna have a house with a tire swing and a vanity and a picket fence, and go on vacations, and be a normal family . . . and then just leave again? What the hell kind of loused-up angel is that?"

His talk of tire swings and picket fences had Lois confused. Had Stephen fed him such ideas? And did he even know what a vanity was? "Stuart, he didn't mean to leave," she said, saving her questions for another day. The important thing now was to find some way into his heart, so she could calm his anger and console him. "God just must have figured he did everything he needed to do down here, and He took him home."

"*We're* his home! The stupid Lord can take him later! Why does God take everything from us? Bad enough our house and all our things! Why couldn't He leave my daddy? What did I do so wrong that He would take my daddy?"

"Baby, come here." She tried to pull him to her, but he twisted away from her.

He screamed at her, "He could have taken anybody! Charles Manson! Old people that already have been around a hundred years. My daddy's only twenty-nine years old!" He grabbed a stack of magazines from the end table and hurled them across the room. "I needed him more than you, God! I needed him more!"

Still screaming, he raced down the hall to Stephen's room. Two nurses were there, disconnecting the tubes.

He stopped short and stared at the bed where Stephen's body lay shrouded in a white sheet. "Daddy!" he cried.

No one except Lidia knew how Stu spent his time over the next couple of days. She knew only because she trailed him, keeping a careful distance between them like a spy in a James Bond movie, so he wouldn't suspect she was there. Except that she wasn't spying on him, despite what he would think if he spotted her. She was being Stu's guardian angel on earth, someone to watch over him until he stopped looking so lost and alone.

She felt sad, too, so sad that her throat ached from the lump that seemed to have gotten stuck there. But when she tried to talk to him about how she felt, he told her to go away and leave him alone.

So she followed him . . . to the quarry . . .

to their old house where he sat for hours in the rubble . . . to the riverbank where he skimmed dozens of pebbles across the water, until her arm began to hurt just from watching him.

Chet and Marsh stopped by the house to visit, but he refused to see them. "He won't speak to anyone," Lidia told them. Not even to her, his very own twin.

"It's a bummer about your dad," said Chet, groping to say the right thing.

"Tell Stu we all feel bad for him and you," Marsh said.

"I'll tell him."

"Tell him the Lipnickis got the fort again. We're going back to claim it. Tell him we need his help," Marsh added.

Chet glared at him. "That's a stupid thing to tell him."

Lidia understood. She didn't know what to say to Stu either. "I'll tell him you came by," she promised.

"Yeah, right," said Marsh.

The boys trudged away. They really did need Stu. None of their usual games were any fun without him.

Stu lay on his bed, gazing blankly at the ceiling. He didn't even blink when Lois knocked on the door and came in.

"The funeral's tomorrow," she said.

His face was a mask. He said, without a flicker of emotion, "I'm not going."

She knew he was hurting, but she was hurting, too, and so was Lidia. Their family needed healing. Closing himself off from them would do no one any good.

"The funeral's tomorrow, and I expect you to be there, young man," she told him.

"What good will it do anyway?" He turned to look at her. "Where will they bury him?"

Lois took the question as a positive omen. It was the first sign of interest he'd had in anything since Stephen's death. She said, "With your grandpa and grandma. I expect you to do right by your father. I know you will."

He got up and left the room. Lois' heart ached to see him go. But he would be at the funeral. She was sure of that.

Lidia was sitting on the stoop when Stu came outside. Not expecting any kind of answer, she asked him, "Where you goin'?"

Much to her surprise, he spoke to her. "Everything's gone, Lidia. Everything."

"I know." She had been thinking the very same thing.

"It's my fault he's dead," said Stu, finally voicing the thought that was haunting him.

Lidia had read about people losing their mind from grief, but she thought that only happened to grownups. "What are you talking about?"

"Because I was fightin'." Stu admitted what was so terribly obvious to him.

It scared Lidia to think her twin might be cuckoo. "That's got nothing to do with why he's dead," she said, wondering if she should run and call her mother.

"Yes, it does. He probably figured out what I did, and he got so disappointed it killed him."

"I did it, too. We all did," said Lidia.

"I ain't blamin' no one. I'm gonna stop it now, before it goes any further," said Stu.

Lidia wasn't exactly sure what he was talking about, but at least he was talking. And he didn't shoo her away when she followed him through the woods. They found Chet, Marsh, and a couple of other boys standing in the field below the fort, which was in bad shape from the assault it had taken.

Several Lipnickis were in the lookout tower, pitching bottles and rocks at the boys, who were halfheartedly returning the fire. Stu waved at his friends but continued walking toward the fort.

"Stu. Don't go there. You'll get creamed," Marsh warned.

The Lipnickis cheered as he approached.

"Simmons, you ready to meet your maker?" Arliss yelled.

"I don't want anything from you," Stu called up to him. "You can have the fort, but I want you all to stop fightin'."

Willard responded to his offer by tossing a melon that bounced off Stu's head. His brothers were laughing so hard they could barely stand up.

"Get out of there, Stu, before they do you in, man," said Chet.

"I ain't leavin' 'till you stop," Stu told the Lipnickis.

"Then you ain't ever leavin'," Arliss said. "Because we sure as hell ain't ever givin' in to you and your kind."

As if to prove his point, the Lipnickis rained down an assortment of missiles on Stu and his friends.

"I have to ask you to stop that now," Stu said calmly, as Lidia and the others scattered for shelter.

Ebb snickered. "And what are you gonna do about it?"

Stu thought of his father facing up to Mr. Lipnicki. He felt very calm. He had his mission, and he was determined to fulfill it.

"I'm gonna get all of you to stop any way I can," he said.

Ebb jumped down from the fort. He came around behind Stu and kicked him in the small of his back, knocking him to the ground. "I stopped," he said.

Lidia, Chet, and Marsh ran to help Stu. The rest of the Lipnickis charged down the ladder and surrounded them.

"I got nothing to fight you with," said Stu, getting to his knees. "You win. Just quit it."

"You don't tell me what to do," shouted Ebb. A second, sharper kick, sent Stu sprawling to the ground yet again.

Stu welcomed the pain. It helped him, he realized as he struggled to pull himself up, to remain focused on his objective.

"You all just get. We'll take care of him." Arliss contemptuously dismissed Stu's friends.

"Don't touch him no more," Lidia yelled, stepping forward to shield her brother.

"Lidia," said Stu. "I don't need no protection. I need for you all to go home and forget all this craziness. Daddy's dead, and none of this means anything. He was right when he said fightin' doesn't make any sense. Go home."

Nobody moved. Of all of them, Lidia was the only one who had any inkling of what he was talking about.

"You heard him. Go home. We'll take care of him," said Arliss.

"Leave him alone. This ain't fair," Billy protested.

Arliss glowered at him. "Billy, I didn't hear no one addressin' you. Pipe down."

"Leave him alone," Billy said, heading toward Stu.

"Shut up!" Arliss pushed him away.

Billy pouted, but the fear of getting a beating from Arliss kept him quiet. Eager to help his new friends, he stared at Stu, then at the fort, then back at Stu. He knew immediately what he needed to do and hustled off to put his plan into action.

"He's got more sense than the rest of you. Just stop. You can have the fort. We'll build another," Stu said, beads of sweat dotting his forehead.

"But they'll nail us wherever we go," Chet wailed.

"That's right," Ebb sang out. He kicked Stu a third time, so viciously that Stu's forehead slammed against the dirt as he pitched forward. "Now get outta here, Simmons."

"Okay. Kick me till you kill me if you have to," Stu gasped. "Because that's the only way I'll leave you be."

His gritty resolve fed Ebb's fury. The brutal seeds that his father's beatings had planted in him erupted in a savage assault to Stu's kidneys.

Stu lay crumpled in the dirt, sobbing and panting for breath. Lidia wept with him, but she didn't dare move to help him up. She vaguely understood that he needed to suffer this much hurt and humiliation because of his guilt for their father's death. She wanted to tell him to stop; he had suffered enough. But she knew he had to work it out for himself.

She watched as he shakily raised himself upright. His nose was bleeding, and he had a gash across his right cheek. His wounds seemed to invite Ebb to yet another attack.

This time, it was Arliss who intervened. "Enough," he said. "The sick bastard likes it when you kick his ass like that. He ain't worth killin'. Go get the others."

Ebb and the other Lipnickis didn't need any more encouragement than that. Arliss was their general; they were his obedient foot soldiers. As ordered, they charged after Lidia and the boys while Stu lay bruised and crying.

"No!" he screamed, though there was no one to hear him.

He crawled to his knees and stared despondently at the fort, and at his friends, running helter-skelter from the Lipnickis. Then his gaze shifted. He gaped at what he thought must be a hallucination. He blinked and looked again; he had not imagined it.

Billy was climbing up the side of the water tower. He was all alone on the ladder, and he was very close to the top.

Drops of blood splattered across Stu's shirt as he lurched to his feet. His lower back was a web of pain. He wasn't sure he could stand, much less run, but he had to stop Billy from hurting himself.

He stumbled across the field to the tower. "Billy! Don't move! Stay there!" he shouted at the tiny figure three quarters of the way up the ladder.

He started up the ladder, climbing as quickly as he could to catch up with Billy. "Hey!" he called. "Wait for me!"

Billy heard him but paid no attention. He continued on his solitary expedition, summoning his strength to pull himself from one rung to the next. Finally, he reached the top.

He stepped onto the platform and made the mistake of looking down. The ground was much further away than he had remembered. He felt so dizzy that he had to close his eyes to keep from falling over. He reminded himself why he was there, which gave him the courage to open his eyes again.

He surveyed the platform until he saw what he had come for. The key to Stu's army lock glinted in the sunlight, just a few feet away.

Even his brothers said that walking the platform was dangerous. Carefully, one step at a time, he crossed the rotting planks. He was getting closer and closer to the key. He could almost feel it in his hand. He could imagine how happy Stu would be when he gave it back to him.

He was enjoying himself now and feeling more confident. He continued onward. A plank creaked ominously. Before he could scramble to safety, it shattered under his foot. He cried out as his left leg ripped through the nylon sheeting that stretched across the top of the platform. He dangled there for a terrifying moment, until he managed to grab hold of another, more solid board and pull himself free.

He got up and steadied himself; his silhouette standing out against the clear blue sky.

Ula saw him first. "Is that Billy climbin' up there by himself?" she yelled.

Arliss looked up an swore, "Oh, shit! Dad's gonna kill us!"

"Who's chasin' him up the thing?" Ebb said.

"That nut Simmons!" Willard exclaimed. "He must have lost his mind."

Lidia and company were instantly forgotten. They sprinted through the woods after Arliss.

"Hey!" he shouted, coming up to the base of the tower. He gestured to Stu, who glanced down, then turned and kept on climbing. Arliss scrambled after him, and the rest of the kids followed.

Billy crept forward on his hands and knees. He was making good progress. He slowly moved closer and closer. Only inches away now, he lay on his stomach and stretched out his arm to grab the key. His fingers brushed it. He was not quite close enough. He stretched his arm further, as far as he could.

A board gave way right next to him. Another board splintered down the middle. His fist closed around the warm metal key. *He had it!* He took a deep breath and raised his hand so the world could see his prize. Then he stuck it in his pocket and got ready for the climb back down.

But before he could take a single step, the wood under his feet suddenly split in half, creating a yawning gap in the surface where one second earlier Billy's weight had been. He plunged through the hole but just barely managed to grab onto one of the planks. He clung to the plank, suspended above the pool, howling in terror.

Stu heard his screams as he climbed over the top of the tower. He moved as quickly as he dared across the platform, covering the last few feet on his hands and knees.

"I'm gettin' your key for the fort," Billy greeted him.

"Hold on!" Stu called. "Don't do anything stupider!"

Arliss got to the top and stepped onto the platform. "If you harm that boy, you're dead meat, Simmons!" he cried, scrambling after him.

Stu kept on moving. "I'm not tryin' to harm him. I'm tryin' to help him."

Arliss overtook him and got to Billy first. He grabbed hold of his arm and said, "It's okay now. I got you."

"I'm scared," Billy sobbed.

"It's okay. Let go," Arliss said, trying to stay

calm. He braced himself with one arm and hauled Billy up with the other. His body had almost cleared the platform when the plank that Arliss was leaning on broke under his weight. He fell backwards and lost his grip.

"No!" Billy screamed and plummeted feet-first into the rushing black waters below.

"No!" Arliss echoed his brother's screams. "No! I had him! I had him!"

"It's okay!" Stu said, panting with fear. "C'mon! We'll get him!"

They were moving so quickly down the interior ladder toward the pool, they almost fell themselves. It took a moment for their eyes to adjust to the darkness. "Billy?" they shouted, scanning the pool. "Billy?"

Stu spotted him first, floating on his back around the outermost edge of the whirlpool. He lay limp and unresistant to the water current.

"There he is!" he called to Arliss. He couldn't tell whether Billy was breathing. He prayed that the boy was still alive.

"I'll get a piece of wood," Arliss yelled and raced up the ladder.

"Hurry!" Stu shouted.

Arliss was back within moments, carrying part of a splintered plank.

Stu hadn't taken his eyes off Billy. He pointed Arliss to him. "He's headin' for the drain."

Arliss bent over the pool and tried to guide Billy with the stick. But he was too far away, and the current was too strong.

"I can't snag him! He ain't movin'! He's drownin', man! What are we gonna do?" he cried.

Stu did what he knew his father would have done. He leapt off the ladder into the swirling eddy. Arliss watched helplessly as Stu chopped through the water toward Billy.

Stu was a strong swimmer, but the icy cold water surged around him, pulling him even closer to the deadly center. A wave hit him in the eyes and momentarily blinded him. He blinked out the water and saw that Billy was now within his reach. He grabbed him under the neck and pulled his head above water. Billy's face was pasty white. He was dead weight in Stu's arms.

He paddled toward the ladder, but the flume kept dragging him backwards. Arliss held out the plank, and after a seemingly endless struggle, Stu managed to grab hold of it. Together they pulled Billy up onto the ladder.

It took some effort to heave him back up to the platform, but between the two of them, they were able to do it. The Lipnickis and Lidia and her friends were waiting for them at the top. Sheer luck had kept them from crashing through the planks, and now they were crowded around the opening, waiting to help the boys drag Billy onto more stable ground.

He still hadn't moved a muscle or opened his eyes. He felt floppy and lax, like an oversized inflatable rubber doll. As far as Stu could tell, he wasn't breathing. His rib cage wasn't moving, and he could feel no air coming out of his nostrils.

He knelt over him and began to administer the

mouth-to-mouth resuscitation technique he learned in his swimming class. Arliss pounded his chest, trying to expel the water he had obviously swallowed. Most of the children were silent; a few were weeping as the boys continued to work on him.

"Oh my God! Billy, you dummy!" Ula sobbed. "What was he doin' down there?"

"Hell if I know!" said Arliss.

"C'mon, Billy," Stu urged, coming up for air. "Help me, now. Take a breath. C'mon, wake up! Goddamnit, Billy! Fight it!"

He slapped his face, to try and shock him back to consciousness. When he got no response, he slapped him again.

"Stop it, you're hurtin' him!" cried Ula.

Two bright red marks showed up against the pale blue pallor of Billy's skin. Arliss stared at his baby brother. He was dead. There was no use believing otherwise. Stuart buried his face in his hands and sobbed unashamedly. Two senseless deaths were more than he could bear.

Then he decided; no, he wasn't going to let Billy die. He bent over him again and resumed the mouth-to-mouth resuscitation.

"It ain't no use," muttered Arliss and burst into tears.

Stu kept on breathing air into Billy's mouth.

"He's gone! Just leave him alone!" said Leo.

Quitters, that's what they were. Just like the damn doctors and nurses in the hospital who had let his father die. Well, he was in charge here, and there wasn't a friggin' chance in hell that he was going to give up on Billy.

"Billy, don't you listen to them!" he whispered. "We're gonna pull through this, you and me."

He picked up where Arliss had left off, pumping Billy's chest. A thin trickle of water spilled out of his mouth.

"I said, leave him be! Just let him go!" Leo cried, pulling him away from Billy.

"No!" Stu sobbed. He pushed Leo out of his way. "He can come back! You gotta give him a chance!"

Sure that Billy could hear him, he kept on talking as he worked to clear more water from his lungs. "I know things have been rough on you, but you got to come back now, you hear? My dad says people can do anything they have a mind to, long as they believe they can. And you're still a little kid, Billy. You believe!" he said fiercely.

A few more drops of water ran out of Billy's mouth, but he still didn't seem to be breathing. "Will somebody please help me?" Stu begged.

Lidia wanted Billy to revive, for his own sake, as well as for Stu's. She bent over his mouth and started the mouth-to-mouth again. "You wake up now, Billy," she told him. "Nobody's gonna be mad at you. You did the best you could. You're a real-life hero."

Seconds passed, and still there was no change. And then suddenly, Billy's legs twitched. A trace of color flowed back into his face. He coughed and threw up a mouthful of water and vomit.

"Holy God," Arliss murmured, with the reverence of someone who had just witnessed his first miracle.

Billy opened his eyes.

"I got the key," he whispered. He stuck his hand in his pocket. After all that, the key was still there. He grinned feebly and handed it to Stu.

"Did you stop the fightin'?" he asked Stu.

Stu shook his head. "No. But you did."

CHAPTER FOURTEEN

Stu and Lidia didn't see much of the Lipnickis after Billy almost drowned. Word had it that they didn't hang around the woods very much anymore. The twins and their friends got to work rebuilding the fort. But after a few days, they all lost interest. The boys discovered girls and began to hang around the movie theater. The girls discovered makeup and started hanging around the makeup counter at Woolworth's, trying to convince the clerks to give them free make-overs.

The week before summer school ended, while they were playing cards on the stoop, a nice-looking man wearing a big-city suit drove up to their house. "Good afternoon. Is your mamma here?" he said.

They brought him inside, where Lois had her school books spread out all over the kitchen table.

"Ma'am." He tipped his hat. "My name is John Ray Wilkens. I'm with the Clariville Auction House?" he said, as if the name should mean something to her.

"Yes?" asked Lois, suddenly worried that he had come to evict them.

"About six weeks ago, your husband put a bid

down on one of our bank-owned properties. We tried to call y'all, but I guess the phone's been down."

Lois' cheeks reddened. She said, "Things have been a little tight."

He nodded understandingly. "Well, anyway," he went on. "A lot of folks start with a minimum bid of five thousand dollars. Not your husband, though. He put a bid down of 432 dollars."

He opened his briefcase and took out an envelope.

"Well, thanks for returnin' the check. We could sure use the money," she said.

"No, ma'am," said Mr. Wilkens. "I'm not here to return the check. You see, the bank took on too many failed mortgages. If they don't start getting rid of their property, they'll soon be facing bankruptcy themselves. The bank accepted your husband's offer . . ."

He chuckled as he handed her the envelope. "Being that it was the only one."

Lois felt certain she had misunderstood him. "Are you tellin' me Stephen bought us a house?" she asked.

Mr. Wilkens smiled with the genuine pleasure of a man who enjoyed delivering good news. "Yes, ma'am. I'm here to deliver the escrow papers and the deed. Would y'all like to come out and take a look at her?" he said.

Would they? They couldn't pile into his car fast enough.

The white frame house was just exactly as Stu remembered it. Lois stared at the picket fence in front and smiled through her tears. She bet there was a vanity in her bedroom, just as she had always wanted.

"Lidia! Come around back. I'll show you a secret way in," Stu called, running to show her the tree with the swing outside his window.

The leaves rustled above his head. He thought he heard his father's voice on the wind. "The next owner is none other than . . . ," the voice was saying.

Lidia came around the corner of the house and stared at the tree swing. "Cool," she said.

"Let me borrow Daddy's angel pen?" he asked.

She gave it to him and went to try out the swing. He carved into the bark, "This here tree belongs to none other than . . . THE SIMMONS FAMILY."

"Thank you, Daddy," he whispered.

On the last day of summer school, Miss Strapford asked for volunteers to read aloud their memoirs. Lidia's hand shot up before anyone else. She had worked hard on her essay. She felt proud of what she had written and wanted everyone to hear it.

"Go ahead, Lidia," said Miss Strapford, who had been considerably nicer to her since her father had died.

Lester Lucket stuck out his tongue when she stood up to read. She paid him no mind at all. Even with all the papers she had written for him, he hadn't passed summer school. He wouldn't be going on to junior high with her and Elvadine. If they were lucky, they might never have to speak to him again.

She stood up straight and tall, and cleared her throat. Then she began to read: "My daddy once said of fightin', we are meant for better things, you and I. And these days, whenever I'm ready to haul off and belt someone who's got my dander up, I hear him whisper those words in my ear.

"My mamma says, people's lives are like tapestries. The color and the beauty of the design depend on all the people you know and the things you've learned. What I learned this summer is that no matter how much people think they understand war, war will never understand people. It's like a big machine that don't nobody really know how to work—and once it gets outta hand, it winds up wreckin' all the things you thought you were fightin' for, and a whole bunch of other good things you sort of forgot you had.

"I learned that my daddy is the wisest man I've ever known. And I learned that no matter what anybody tells you, with God's help, human beings can do anything."